THE MIGHTY FALL

THE MIGHTY FALL

A Tale of Brotherhood, War, & Trauma

A NOVEL BY

Grace Godfrey

SMALL BATCH BOOKS
Amherst, Massachusetts

Printed in the United States of America

ISBN: 978-1-951568-35-1
Library of Congress Control Number: 2023910727

Images on title page from iStock photo: Johncairns and Rouzes

Designed by Mary A. Wirth

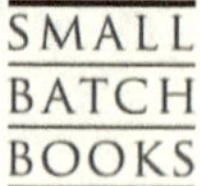

493 South Pleasant Street
Amherst, Massachusetts 01002
413.230.3943
smallbatchbooks.com

Dedicated to Ray Falconer, my eigth grade English teacher.
Thank you for always believing in me and laying
the groundwork for my love of writing.

PROLOGUE

"Need I remind you why you're here?"

There was little humanity inside the dim, moist underground trolley. Three men—barbarians, perhaps—stood tall and proud against the back of the trolley. The space felt devoid of life, and death seemed imminent. Everyone tried to stay focused on the task at hand, but the spent lights, which flickered on and off to a seemingly random rhythm, refused to comply. Water dripped through the rusting steel and ran its course quietly to the middle of the room. Everyone was silent except for the fourth man, whose whimpering bounced on and off the walls in an endless loop of plea and fear wound into a single sound.

"Need I remind you why you're here?" The same voice blanketed the whimper. The three men standing overshadowed the fourth.

"No." The fourth man straightened up, as best he could, and ceased whimpering as a newfound energy zipped through the room. Simultaneous collisions of hope and despondency whizzed around in the fourth man's voice, a whimper no more. The lights, as if supernaturally sensing the increased energy, switched on, no longer flickering. The men inside blinked to compensate for the sudden burst of light. The scene came into view.

Three men dressed in navy blue suits and purple ties stood around a chair. Tied by rope, but bound by fear, sat a man wearing a black suit and a white tie. His face oozed blood from a trauma above his eyelid, yet his eyes remained intact, counterintuitively shining. The fourth man heard what he thought was a horse and chuckled. "Need I remind you you're too late?" he sneered.

The three men, already looking at the fourth man with disdain, clenched their jaws. The tallest of them cocked his gun. The water dripped faster with the sound of horses running above. Only the fourth man looked up. The other three remained still, like proud statues, circling the chair on which the fourth man forcefully sat.

"Easy, comrade. We need him alive. For Crail, remember?"

The tallest man holstered his gun. The fourth man shook his head and bit his tongue. Clearly, he was smart enough not to speak in a room that demanded silence. Neither the three Crail men, nor the sole Burfordian, said a word. The only sound that could be heard was the cacophony of the streets aboveground, muffled by layers of dirt. And even that was uneventful, people going about their day, knowing somewhere beneath them, life and death were playing with each other. Yet, that was commonplace in these times, times when survival was more important than sanity.

"You crossed a line, Mr. Jameson. . . ."

Words cut through the demands for silence. They echoed off each surface and straight into Alistair Jameson's ears. The words bounced in his brain, forcing his cells to awaken and work properly, to comprehend life and death in this moment, as his shining eyes spun, patiently awaiting further command.

". . . You're a liar. . . ."

Alistair sat still, watching the lights, which had resumed flickering, and the water, which raced down its invisible slide into the puddle forming at his feet. Of course, there was nothing he could do but sit and watch the random distractions as he silently planned his next course of action.

". . . You and your lot from Burford."

At this, Alistair looked up, his silent demeanor trying to hold him back, trying to stop him from speaking. His black pelt of stealth and patience began to fade, and some specks of pure human flesh began poking their way to the surface.

"We have a name, Mr. Dirkson. . . ."

The black pelt faded completely, and he could not remain silent any longer. The malice woven into Alistair's response floated in the air, up for grabs for those who were listening. Perhaps the horses above felt the malice, too, as they all came to a sudden stop. The people, as well, perhaps noticing what the horses did, hushed down and scurried off. Everything seemed calm, aboveground that is. Not even the claws of poverty nor the jaws of necessity were enough to keep the beggars above begging. No one said a thing. No one except the four men underground in a trolley car. Ironic, isn't it? The threat of death spurs on the thrill of life.

". . . We have a name. . . ."

Alistair's eyes tackled Dirkson's, and those of the other three men brave, or stupid, enough to make eye contact with Alistair's killer stare.

". . . and I know you 'lot' know it."

In the way Alistair carried himself, despite the fact that he was restrained, he seemed bigger. He had a stare that could bring death out of the grave and life to its knees. Even sitting, strapped to a chair with an open wound, he could kill a lion with a mere glance in its direction. Dirkson, on the other hand, had a sensitive stare. Instead of eyeing the world as an offensive mission, like the likes of Alistair, he saw the world as an opportunity to gain reconnaissance. Although nothing about Dirkson was delicate. Even his gun that lay safely in his holster carried the weight of a thousand men. Maybe he had the Midas Touch. Nevertheless, when two heavyweights clash, it ends in a bang.

"We're dreamers, Mr. Jameson."

The water, now crawling up Alistair's loafers, began to thin out to almost no drops. Every other minute or so, a single drop would fatefully sail alone into a madhouse of water that soon encircled the lone drop and waited for its next prey to fall victim. Dirkson glanced at his two cronies. They both nodded, united from a well-thought-out glance.

"You're drunk on dreams, Mr. Dirkson."

The trolley filled with an indescribable chill. The kind of chill that runs down one's spine, tickling the flesh. The kind of chill that makes the hairs on the back of the neck stand on end. An uneasy warmth soon followed, producing a repulsive draft. The men looked around in a pointless attempt to identify the source. Perhaps all of their roots were rotting, giving off an aura even the naked eye could sense. Underneath the svelte layers of felt and cotton, humanity, in its rawest form, was exposed. But these four distinguished gentlemen needed something to distinguish them; something to cover their humanity with. Perhaps as a self-protective measure, a way in which they could forget about their barbaric, or angelic, nature.

"We dream about the future. . . . You, Mr. Jameson, you are stuck in the past."

Alistair calmly turned his head, eyeing each of the men in navy blue suits and purple ties. There is something to be said about Alistair's own black suit and white tie. The contrast of black and white is very much like that of defeat and victory.

"Au contraire, Mr. Dirkson . . ."

Even the repulsive draft and the established hostile tone wasn't intimidating enough for Alistair to add some light into the conversation. In the mouth of darkness, he laughed, and in the heart of purity, he frowned. Mr. Dirkson, on the other hand, was having none of it. He took a step toward Mr. Jameson, careful not to look him in the eye. Mr. Dirkson now stood a length in front of his comrades. A clear hierarchy emerged. Of course, humanity is a hierarchy. What it means to be human means to rank, list, and sort everything. A hierarchy exists everywhere, in everything. Aboveground, where it was alarmingly quiet, a pecking order was as clear as day. The beggars, the homeless, the street workers, and the homeless widows donned ripped, old, and tired clothing. They were the first to wake and last to eat. Yet underneath them stood some of the wealthiest people in England, even for a time like this. Funny how these four men not afraid of the daylight only see the darkness.

". . . we are dreamers too . . . only we say we're idealists. And you know where you fail, Mr. Dirkson?"

In normal circumstances, failure isn't fatal. But in high-stakes circumstances, like war, failure is costly. Failure to win translates to casualties. Failure to know what losing is translates to casualties.

"We don't fail."

"Yes, you do, Mr. Dirkson." Alistair's humorous tone from before completely faded. His killer stare once again made its way to the front of his icy blue eyes. Everything that looked into that unforgiving stare melted away. Maybe that's why the water stopped dripping and the lights stopped flickering. Maybe that's why the horses above stopped running. Speaking of, some footsteps could be heard aboveground. The steps were quick yet confident. Nothing about them fit in with the sad and weak steps of the poor Crail civilians.

"You see, you, Mr. Eastaughffe and Mr. Cromwell . . ."

Neither of those men said anything verbal, although their bodies were busy chatting. It was Oliver Eastaughffe who had pulled out his gun and nearly shot Alistair. But Eastaughffe, a looming presence to behold, spoke with his motions, or lack thereof, all evening. He didn't move an inch since arriving in the trolley car, and he barely looked away from Alistair. Like an osprey, he knew prey when he saw it. But like an alligator, sometimes he went for prey too big. Although, in this underground trolley, the limits of big and small have seemingly disintegrated into one size.

". . . aren't kin, . . ."

Eastaughffe still did not react to Alistair's words. In part because he knew what Alistair said was true; they weren't related. The familial bonds, whether good or bad, connect all of humanity. Muggers, murderers, train conductors, farriers, doctors, and Parliament all have one thing in common: family. It can only be assumed that to him, family is a nightmare that resurfaces every day.

". . . but me and my 'lot' are family. . . ."

The busy chatter from the people above the ground all of a sudden resumed as the confident footsteps vanished. Noise from every corner flooded the streets in a massive avalanche of sound. The beggars were back to begging, the muggers back to mugging, the common folk back to shopping. It was as if someone unleashed hundreds of people, starved from speaking for hundreds of days. As a result of the chaos aboveground, the water started dripping again and lights began to dully flicker. It was as if the lights and the water were holding their breath, not wanting to miss a single part of the drama in the underground trolley car. The only thing that couldn't be heard were the horses.

". . . and my family looks after family." The lights suddenly quit, and darkness quickly dominated the room. Not that any of the men were afraid; they were too used to the dark to fear it. Eastaughffe, of course, still didn't move, but he took the opportunity to look directly at Alistair. Only in complete darkness did Alistair's killing stare spare peoples' lives. The water droplets, ricocheting off the steel floor, made an even louder sound than before. It was as if the whole compartment tensed up.

"Enough, Mr. Jameson." The angry voice of Mr. Dirkson hit the steel hard and bounced back hard. It clashed with the darkness in an attempt to be the scariest thing in the room. His voice wanted to be number one—humanity's desire to rank. All of humankind wants to be better than the natural, better than the darkness, the forests, the ocean, and all things people find terrifying. Humanity must be number one in every category, even the ones that nobody is proud of. When there's competition to be number one, humanity crushes any resistance. But what happens when the competition is an internal battle, human versus human conflict? War.

"Family looks after family." Suddenly, a new sound emerged. A sound very close, as if it were just outside the trolley car. *Click.* The unmistakable sound of a gun cocking. Mr. Jameson smiled and let out a low laugh. "Mr. Dirkson, Mr. Eastaughffe, and Mr. Cromwell, I'm sure you know my brothers."

Indeed, there were now six men underground. Mr. Dirkson reached for his gun but stopped. He knew it was pointless. The Jameson brothers had come to rescue their kidnapped brother.

"Let my brother go." One of the brothers pointed his gun directly at Dirkson's head. Dirkson looked at Cromwell, who, very slowly, bent down and untied Alistair, who stood and calmly walked toward the safety of his brothers.

"Oh, gentlemen, one last thing . . ." He stopped and turned his head just enough to see over his shoulder. Dirkson, Eastaughffe, and Cromwell stood, shocked that their operation hadn't worked, defeatedly looking at the ground. Only Dirkson raised his head to look Alistair in the eyes, as if to say, *Next time, you'll die.*

". . . the name is the Brassy Gats."

THE MIGHTY FALL

CHAPTER 1

Alistair Jameson sat at his desk in a refurbished warehouse. He had been watching his clock tick with each changing second for hours. He was supposed to be writing a letter, but he couldn't think of anything to say. It had been nearly two months since his run-in with his Crail counterparts, and he couldn't stop thinking about the whole incident. He had other things to worry about, things like business and his youngest brother, Davenport. Davenport had been getting into trouble lately. He had a temper he couldn't control, consumed unlimited amounts of alcohol, and had ways to avoid getting arrested. Alistair sighed and looked down at his blank sheet of paper. He reached for his pen and gathered his thoughts. He would've preferred to call—after all, it was 1930 and the telephone was as modern as ever—but he knew spies could be listening, and he needed confidentiality. Slowly, he began to let his ideas guide his pen across the paper, and he formulated maybe the most important letter of his life.

Dear Mr. Alcott Dirkson,

The date is August 3rd, 1930. I'm writing to you with concerns about an incident in Conwy. I was surprised, at first, at the distance you and the rest of your group were willing to go to undermine my operations. But it soon occurred to me that your ambitions are great, and no distance will stop you. But I must warn you, Mr. Dirkson, that I haven't forgotten about our little encounter last June. As such, there will be no tolerance for your business in Conwy. I've given my men permission to rid the city of you, in any way they deem necessary, in two days' time if your men haven't completely left. I've also put my brother Davenport in charge of the operations in Conwy.

You and I are the same person, Mr. Dirkson. We're money men, making money in any way we can. As ideas come into my head, they become reality, hence why we are idealists and you are dreamers. So I suggest that you and your dreams vacate the Conwy area and find some other port. This is an island surrounded by water, and I reckon finding another port shouldn't be hard. Especially for a man with your wit. You know what's best, Mr. Dirkson, and failure to adhere to my demands will result in casualties. You and I fought in the trenches for our country, so I know you understand when I tell you this: Leave, or I'll make you.

Best regards,
Alistair Jameson,
Brassy Gats

"Mary, can you come here? I have a letter for you to mail." Alistair's assistant came in from the hall.

"Yes, sir." She gingerly reached out, took the letter from his hands, then quietly turned and left his office. The letter would reach Alcott Dirkson later that evening, as Alistair has connections in the mail service.

The phone rang, startling Alistair. He instantly grabbed the phone and answered, his heart starting to beat faster.

"Hello?"

"Alistair, you're needed right away. There's been a shooting"—Alistair's brother Bradley was out of breath—"at the race track—"

"Easy, brother, calm down. Who's been shot?"

"Not a who, Ally, a what. King Dream has been killed."

"No!" Alistair hung up the phone, grabbed his jacket, and raced off. He practically jumped down the staircase and flew out of the headquarters in the warehouse. He sprinted down the street toward Burford Downs, the horse track. Today was supposed to be a great day for his company. Today the favorite, King Dream, was going to lose. And everyone who put their money on him was going to lose it to the Brassy Gats. Alistair knew that for a fact.

"Mr. Jameson!" Alistair nearly ran into Ellenore, his horse trainer. A female trainer was unusual, but Alistair thought she was the best he ever had. She was frazzled; her normally neatly tucked hair was wildly out of place. Her elegant jumpsuit was tainted with blood spatter, and she held her boots in her hand. Her feet were muddy and scraped from running all the way from Burford Downs barefoot. She reached out and grabbed Alistair. He took her by the arm and they both resumed running as fast as they could back to the track.

"What happened?"

"I tried to stop him, I did! But he said if I didn't let him see the horse, he'd put a bullet in my son's head. Oh, I'm so sorry, Mr. Jameson!"

"Breathe, Ellenore, breathe. It's all right. Did you get a good look at him?" Alistair took a couple of quick, sharp breaths. He was out of breath from sprinting, but he needed to get to the racetrack. More importantly, he needed to know who was behind that attack, although he already had a feeling he knew.

"I'll never forget his face."

"Good." After that, the two ran in silence. Now that he was without a racehorse, Alistair's profits would be solely coming from the port in Conwy. The same place his rivals needed to survive too.

"They're positive the stallion is dead?"

Ellenore just glanced up at Alistair. Her cunning green eyes were filled with a glossy sadness. A look was all they needed to communicate the atrocity at Burford Downs.

"Who would shoot a horse, Mr. Jameson, who? I've seen men die, but horses? They go down hard—it's heartbreaking."

"A barbarian, Ellenore, a barbarian."

A large, usually pleasant sign, came into view. The colorful lights gave no hint of the blackness inside. Under normal circumstances, it would've filled Alistair with joy, but these weren't normal circumstances. The stakes were high.

"Wait out here, Ellenore. I'll have someone pick you up and take you back home." She nodded and collapsed to the ground. Her heart broke at the lack of humanity she had witnessed today.

"Mr. Jameson! We've got the place locked down, but no sign of the shooter," Johnny, the owner of the race track, reported.

"No one leaves without being searched."

"Already done, Mr. Jameson."

"Good, Johnny, good." Alistair put his hands on his thighs and tried to calm his breathing. He focused on a small pebble that lay in the dirt in front of him. Suddenly, a large gust of wind picked up and carried the pebble away. He watched as it rolled into the tall grass. Funny how something so dense and so hard was easily carried away by something light and swift.

"Johnny, new orders." Alistair put his hand in the air to signal Johnny to stay put. "Take Ms. Rose back to her house. She's had a rough day." He glanced back at her. She had collected herself somewhat, but she still couldn't take her eyes away from the racetrack.

"Ms. Rose, sir?" Alistair sighed and pointed back at Ellenore. Johnny nodded and began making his way toward her. Alistair looked up to the heavens and grunted. He shook his head, collected his thoughts, and jogged into Burford Downs. The whole place was in hubbub, yet no horses were out racing and no bartenders were pouring people drinks.

"Alistair! Ally!" Alistair looked around. He spotted his brother Bradley wildly waving his arms in an attempt to get Alistair's attention. In Bradley's right hand was a gun. Remembering that somewhere on the premises there was a man carrying a revolver, Alistair also reached for his gun, nestled safely in his side holster, and grabbed it. He raced down the stairs and jumped the barrier separating the people from the track. With each step he felt the ground getting colder, the scent of death getting stronger. Once he reached Bradley, he kept on running till he was dead center of the track. Cocking his gun, he fired it straight up. People all throughout the course gasped and turned their heads to look at Alistair. The chatter instantly stopped as fear crept in. These are the clean, rich folks; they aren't used to the sound of a gun firing.

"One of you bastards in this racetrack killed an innocent horse! One of you killed *my* horse! And one of you is going to pay for it! I can guarantee that when the Brassy Gats find you, it'll be you with the bullet through your head! I'll shoot you myself!" Alistair was livid not only because of what had happened to his horse, but also because he knew what was going to happen next. His city now had a major vulnerability, and everything Alistair had worked so hard for balanced on only one leg; a human on one leg can't afford gusts of wind, or they'll be dragged down, just like the pebble.

"Easy, Ally, easy. I've called Davenport and—"

"Tell Davenport to stay where he is. He must remain in Conwy, you hear me? At all costs he must stay put."

"He's not going to like that, Ally. You know he wants to be in the middle of these kinds of things."

"He'll soon be in the middle of something bigger, Brad." Alistair turned, holstered his gun, and solemnly walked away from Bradley toward his fallen horse. There had been no need for such a bold act of anger. As leader, he should've approached this in a calmer fashion. He grabbed a toothpick from his breast pocket and began to chew it, but he bit right through it. Tiny splinters of wood floated around in his mouth. He leaned over and spit it out, getting another from his pocket.

Alistair defeatedly trotted back to his brother, back to the safety of his family.

"Mr. Jameson!" Alistair turned his head. A man dressed in farrier clothes was running, full speed, toward him. Alistair recognized him right away.

"Tommy. I told you to call me Alistair. We fought together in France, comrade." Alistair slapped the farrier on the shoulder in a manly display of affection. It was an attempt to blanket the biting winds and unforgiving silence.

"Right, Alistair, you've got a call. It's—"

"Let me guess, Davenport?" Tommy nodded and told Alistair that Davenport sounded mad. And drunk. Mad and drunk. Alistair nodded and took off jogging toward the stands to get to the phone. He knew Davenport was always mad and always drunk. But it was surface emotions to cover up the rawness that was eating away at him. Alistair knew Davenport had died in the war. No one came back the same man they were before, but Davenport especially. Davenport was a decorated soldier; he had won two gallantry medals. But that had come at a high price. Davenport was the only Jameson brother who hadn't been in the same platoon. He was also the only tunneler in the family, and it showed. His physical scars were obvious, with a large slanting mark disrupting the purity of his face, but his emotional ones also ran deep. The only time Davenport had been stationed with his brothers was the worst time of Alistair's life. Alistair nearly lost two brothers that day.

"Mr. Jameson, a phone call for you, sir." Alistair hadn't even noticed he'd climbed into the stands and stood amongst the terrified civilians at the racetrack, who all avoided him. He reached out and grabbed the phone from the bartender, who quickly scurried away.

"Ally! I heard what happened, are you all right?" Davenport was out of breath, panting like he'd just been running. More likely, he was terrified.

"Yes, Davy. But I need you to stay there. It'll all make sense in due course."

"No way! Why should I be left out of this? I helped establish our monopoly over fixed races. Why can't I be there when we find that son of a bitch who killed the horse?"

"Listen to me. If you come here, I'll take away your position in

Conwy. This is a direct order. Stay exactly where you are and carry on with usual operations. Oh, and don't forget about the Crail men. They have two days to leave before you have the right to expel them."

"Why, Ally? What's so important that I have to stay here, helpless, while you and Brad have to deal with this on your own? You know we're stronger together!"

"Calm down, Davenport!"

"Don't tell me to calm down, Alistair!" Alistair was taken aback by the sound of his full name. Only his brothers called him Ally. He hated it when they called him Alistair. All he needed to be for his family was a brother. All he needed to be was himself. Historically, the name Alistair was a warrior name, meaning "the one who repels men." He didn't want to be a warrior in the comfort of his own home. He just wanted to be Ally, the man who could fail without causing casualties. The man who was man enough just being a human.

"Listen, Davy. You know we need Conwy. We need to protect it from Crail—"

"From the Snappy Kings? I know that."

"Look, if we lose Conwy to the Snappy Kings, we lose our export of gin to America. If we lose our exportation, we lose our money. We can't afford that. So do as you're told and remain where you are. Old soldiers never die, remember." Davenport sighed and Alistair heard him cover his mouth with his hand.

Alistair hung up the phone. He put his hands on the bar table and breathed deeply, trying to calm himself. He feared the worst; he feared an all-out war with the rival gang. But he had already lived through the tortures of war, and he refused to experience that again. He vowed, right there, to at least try to end this conflict diplomatically. He wasn't optimistic, but he had to try. He rolled up his sleeve to reveal a scar, spanning from his elbow down to his wrist. He closed his eyes in an attempt to free himself from reality, but he only brought the memories of war to the forefront of his mind. Shuddering, he opened his eyes. He had kept memories of the war locked away for so many years, just like every other man. He glanced back at the scar. It was a reminder of his sacrifice for his country.

"Ally"—Bradley put his hand on his brother's shoulder—"everyone's been searched. No sign of the gun. Shall I let our men open the doors?" Alistair looked up and slowly nodded. Even though they couldn't find the weapon, he knew the horse slayer was in the building. In many ways, the shooter was like Gavrilo Princip; depending on the side, Princip was either a barbarian or an angel. But ultimately Princip caused a war, and Alistair made it his goal to prevent war between his Brassy Gats and Crail's Snappy Kings. He knew that's what his Crail counterparts wanted, and he couldn't give them that glory.

"Oh, Brad?"

"Yeah?"

"Old soldiers never die." Bradley stopped and turned around. He reached out and hugged his brother close. He and Alistair remained in the embrace for what seemed like forever. Alistair rested his head on his younger brother's shoulder. Taller than most, at six feet six, Bradley made even Mr. Eastaughffe's six-foot-three looming presence quiver.

"Old soldiers never die," Bradley whispered back.

"You know what this means, right, Brad?"

Bradley nodded his head. He explained that killing the horse was the smartest move their enemy could've made. It forced them to either fight for Conwy or run dry. In an era when money was sparse, those who had it would die defending it.

Suddenly, Alistair pushed away from his brother's warmth, and almost instantly his spine crawled with an unmistakable chill. The same chill he felt months prior in the trolley car. "It's just a horse, brother. Let's not get overly sentimental?" He slapped Bradley on the back in an attempt to bring some energy into the conversation.

"Yeah, yeah, you're right."

Alistair straightened up and turned around, heading for his office back in the warehouse. But in his mind he could only think of one thing: *Old soldiers never die.* Soldiers who fought in the Great War twelve years ago were becoming increasingly forgotten. The rest of the proverb—*old soldiers never die, they simply fade away*—is humanity's way of attempting to protect itself. By forgetting about the men who died, or survived, for their country, humanity could forget the pain, carnage, and embarrassment of the war. But Alistair ignored the latter half of the phrase. Those four words held more importance to Alistair than a lot of things.

"What now, Alistair?" Alistair looked up and realized he had been pointlessly wandering in circles and nearly collided with Tommy.

"We protect Conwy, Tommy. We protect Conwy at all costs."

"That's not going to be easy."

"We don't have a choice." Alistair put his hands in his trench coat pockets and walked out of Burford Downs.

The blue sky that started the day rolled into an overcast gray. Even nature sensed the unfortunate situation.

A storm was brewing, and it would bring a trail of destruction with it.

CHAPTER 2

"Daddy!" Alistair looked up from his desk. Bounding in came his six-year-old daughter, Esme. Her long black hair, which very much resembled her late mother's, was neatly tied back into two ponytails. She was very small for her age, but what she lacked in size she made up for in energy. For something so small, she brought the biggest joy in Alistair's life. Nothing made him happier than Esme, not even his brothers. He leaped up from his chair, picked up Esme, and spun her around. Just watching her tiny mouth get bigger and bigger with joy made his heart grow. Her little laugh filled the room with a pleasant warmth, wiping it clean of any despair. Not all is bad, no. Esme made everything better. She was like the gold at the end of the rainbow. Even if the rainbow sagged or faded, the pot of gold was always there, shining like heaven itself. There was no question about it: Esme was an angel.

"I'm sorry, Mr. Jameson, she sprinted so fast, I couldn't catch her. I know you're busy, sir."

"No, Mary, it's quite fine. She can stay with me. My beautiful princess, what shall we do now?"

"Horsey!" Alistair laughed and got down on all fours. Esme playfully hopped on his back and shouted, "Giddyup!" He forgot about his fallen horse and completely transformed into someone new, someone with a smile. The smile that Esme constantly reminded him he had. Smiling is a miraculous thing; peace begins with a smile. Because of his smile, his internal hurricane melted away into the glowing sky, peaceful and calm. A warm smile is the universal language of love and happiness. The whole world could look at Alistair now and know the eternal joy he unleashed into his bloodstream.

The phone rang, and Alistair was forced back into reality. "Esme, I have to take this call. More horsey later?"

"Yeah!" She jumped off his back and skipped out of his office. She was always happy, her innocence still intact, and he selfishly hoped it would always remain intact. But he knew that in order to survive, she needed to know survival skills, skills that are only gained through trying and failing in life's game. If one wants to beat the game, one's got to deal with the twists and turns.

"Hello?"

"Alistair, are you all right? I heard that there was a shooting in Burford." Alistair recognized the man at the end of the line instantly. His unmistakable Italian accent wove its way between the heart of his words. His passion for life was heard, clear as day, in the seconds he'd spoken for. It was a voice Alistair could never hate.

"Yes, Father Romano. Nobody was hurt. My racehorse was shot." Alistair's heart felt at peace when Father Romano spoke to him. He had been his only source of light for a while, before Esme was born. Father Romano was a devout pacifist; he'd sooner die than pick up a gun. In the war, he was deployed with Alistair and the other thirty-two men in his platoon, and he bravely ventured into the trenches with no weapon and no body armor. He'd walk around the trenches day and night, reading prayers, singing hymns, helping the doctors with the wounded soldiers, and comforting the terrified men who just wanted to go home. Alistair thought Father Romano was the bravest man in the whole platoon, and he didn't need a machine gun to make himself known.

His words were perfection. Father Romano just spoke from his heart, and the heart is the most dangerous weapon of them all.

"Thank you for checking in, Father Romano."

"Just doing my job, Alistair."

Alistair smiled. Father Romano was the last of a dying breed. He cared about everyone, and he constantly called the remaining fifteen men who once made up Alistair's mighty platoon. And Davenport. Father Romano called Davenport nearly every day. It was Davenport who had suffered the most during the war. Davenport didn't like to talk about his life as a tunneler, nor the war in general. Davenport suffered from shell shock. Little things that never bothered Davenport now caused him to go into a massive frenzy. In fact, that's the reason the Brassy Gats were stationed in a warehouse: Davenport needed to be able to see all four walls of the warehouse or he'd panic. And the reason so many lights covered the ceiling: Davenport feared the darkness. And it's understandable—the tunnelers in the World War rarely saw the light of day. Alistair knew that Davenport nearly died many times. He also knew that many times Davenport was forced into brutal hand-to-hand combat in the already unstable tunnels. And that the tunnels collapsed onto Davenport at least three times, and each time, Davenport was the only one who made it out alive. They called him "The Iron Man," because Davenport never seemed to die. And because Davenport was always brave. He never put himself before his comrades, and he never gave up. It was Davenport who saved Bradley's life, even though Davenport was the youngest brother. Alistair was four years older and Bradley was two years older. The one day that Davenport emerged from the tunnels was the day he saved Bradley's life. But none of the Jameson brothers talked about that day, not because of the life Davenport saved, but because of the life Davenport couldn't save.

"Father? Have you talked to Bradley recently?"

"Yes, as a matter of fact, I spoke to him not ten minutes ago. He asked about my congregants, then told me to call Davenport, but I couldn't reach him. Then I caught wind of the shooting and called you. How have you been, Alistair?"

"Just dandy, Father, just dandy."

"Keep your head up, Lieutenant." The line went silent after that, and Alistair realized Father Romano had hung up. Alistair sighed and sat down in his chair. He had a big decision to make, but he desperately needed Alcott's response. Alistair didn't fancy waiting around for his enemy. If he was to be self-reliant, he surely need not act dependent on the Snappy Kings. That's how they got their name; their irritable nature mixed with their tendency to idolize monarchical figures. At least the man who started the Snappy Kings' operations was self-aware enough to know how petulant he was. Alistair's thoughts were interrupted by a knock on the door. He dragged his mind from the past to the present.

"Sir, sorry to bother you, but you have a letter." This is what he was waiting for.

"Thank you, Mary." She placed the letter on his desk, gave a curt nod, and left to make biscuits with Esme. Alistair grabbed the letter and tore it open like a madman. His eyes read faster than he thought humanly possible, and he soon realized he was reading too fast for his brain to catch up. He took three deep breaths and quieted his nerves. Then he reread the letter from the beginning.

August 6, 1930

Dear Mr. Alistair Jameson,

Mr. Jameson, how wonderful a surprise it was to receive a letter from you.

Let's get right down to business. Conwy, however vital to your organization, is vital for mine as well. I've been told about your racehorse, Mr. Jameson. Under these current circumstances, I deem it right to believe you won't be fixing races anytime soon, so what option does that leave you and your motley crew with? My men won't be leaving Conwy anytime soon; however, I've told them to stand down until our exchanges cease. I suggest you do the same.

Mr. Jameson, I quite resent the decision to put Davenport

in charge. Everyone knows the crazed man your brother can morph into, and I think it is intentional to intimidate me into leaving. That's not very nice, is it, Mr. Jameson?

Yes, I fought in France, but not in your platoon. We only worked together in the Battle of Somme, if you recall. If I remember right, Mr. Jameson, it was the only battle your brother fought with you and Bradley. There was one more, right? That must be hard on Davenport knowing the consequences of saving Bradley. See, I am an only child, Mr. Jameson. I will never know the pain of losing a brother.

To conclude, my men won't attack yours in Conwy, given that you and I negotiate the situation there, and that you adhere to my demands, which will be sent soon after I finalize them with my colleagues. After all, you aren't in much of a position to decline.

Best Regards,
Alcott Dirkson,
Snappy Kings

Alistair breathed deeply and flared his nostrils. He knew Mr. Dirkson was right. He didn't have a choice. He was already on thin ice with his enemy, hence why he ended up underground in the trolley car. He knew he didn't have any leverage. He spun his chair around and watched the sun gently rest. The gray colors of the soft rain had ceased to dim the bright sky. The warm colors of the evening glistened in the lightness of the clouds. Everything the pastel lights touched settled in a state of eternal peace. The light loved all, hugged all, and calmed all. In many ways, Esme is a reflection of that light. Esme comes from the Old French *esmer*, "to love." His daughter was a perfect blend of humanity and nature wound into a bubbly personality, just like the glittering sunset. Nature has a funny way of sneaking into one's heart, eliminating the pain and breathing life back into it. Nature can't be duplicated; it's too complex, too pure. To Alistair, Esme was the only exception. Nature flows through her veins and colors her eyes a deep natural hazel. In watching the lights of nature dance in the sky, Alistair could lose his worries and simply relax. No one felt that more than the soldiers.

All of a sudden, Alistair jumped to his feet. He needed to deliver the message to Davenport not to shoot.

"Operator? 321 Sychnant Pass Road." Alistair held his breath as he waited for Davenport to answer. Finally, Alistair heard a voice at the end of the line.

"Hello?" It wasn't Davenport.

"To whom am I speaking?"

"Wilcot Randy. Are you calling for Mr. Jameson?"

"Indeed I am, Mr. Randy. May I ask where he is? It's very important."

"He's not here, may I take a message?"

Alistair slammed his fist down on the table. In order to maintain the shaky peace, he needed Davenport to understand the importance of holding his fire. "Where'd he go?"

"Who's asking?" Wilcot sounded angry. Alistair sensed Wilcot was hiding something.

"His brother." There was a sigh from Wilcot, followed by silence. Alistair kept the phone glued to his ear, trying to hear what was happening.

"Ally?" Alistair, startled, dropped the receiver. He put his hand on his chest and chuckled.

"You scared me, Davy."

"Ally, I have to tell you something."

"It's going to have to wait." Alistair heard Davenport groan in complaint. "There's something I need you to understand. There's been a change in plans. Your new orders are to stand down, and do not, I repeat, do not instigate a fight between us and the Snappy Kings. Understood?"

"Why?"

Alistair rolled his eyes. He knew Davenport would obey, but Alistair didn't know how much of what was happening he wanted to tell Davenport. He would update Bradley later, but Davenport often acted impulsively, and Alistair couldn't afford for that to happen.

"Because I said so. They aren't going to fire at you either. Oh, what was it you had to tell me?"

"Nothing." Davenport mumbled and hung up the phone. There was little Alistair could do to reassure his brother he wasn't excluding him, merely restricting him. Alistair wished he could have Davenport close to him at all times, but not only would the responsibility be too great, but Davenport also needed his independence. Alistair couldn't worry about Davenport forever, and right now he had to call Bradley. He would've rather sent a letter, but he hadn't the time.

"Operator, 12 Barns Lane, Burford." The operator told Alistair to hold as she connected him through. The phone rang but once before Bradley picked up.

"Ally?"

"Brad, before we talk business, have you called Davy recently?"

"No, why, what's happened?"

"Nothing, but he has a butler or something like that, a Wilcot Randy. Get your friends on Randy right away. I want every piece of information on him."

"Of course."

"Okay, business now. I've received a letter from Alcott Dirkson. There's no way he's going to leave Conwy peacefully. We're going to have to fight him for that."

"Go figure." Alistair could hear Bradley's eyes roll. He felt the same way.

"I want the men at the lookout in the north transported instantly to Conwy. Dirkson said his men wouldn't fight ours, but we've just gotta be careful."

"Right away. I'll call them the instant this phone call is done."

"Good, thank you. And Bradley, how's the leg?" Alistair could hear Bradley sigh. Alistair knew Bradley was embarrassed. Ever since the war, Bradley's thigh randomly tightened, and it ranged in severity from mild to the point where Bradley couldn't walk.

"Good, good. You know, me and my leg wouldn't be here if it weren't for Davy. We don't talk about this enough. Davy needs to remember that he was, and still is, a hero instead of a killer.

Believe me, it hurts me to think about it. But if one wants to pick a rose, they've got to deal with the thorns." Alistair put his head down. An uncomfortable silence filled the room. It poured from the phone like a dying volcano. The grief was hot and quick, speeding into the room and filling every crevice. Alistair reached up and wiped his eyes. There was no forcing the tears back into his eyes; once it's out, it's out.

"Brad. We don't talk—"

"No, Ally, listen to me. Without Davy, there would be no me. Without Davy, I'd be dead"—suddenly Bradley started weeping—"and I'd be up in heaven. Davy needs to know he saved my life. Without him, it'd be a party of two in heaven." Alistair put his head down and wept with his brother.

"You're right. We have to talk to him about that day."

"And the war in general. He's seen more of humanity's evil than us combined. We saw the devil's teeth from its snarl, but he was inside the mouth, on the edge of being consumed."

"You're right." Alistair took a series of sharp breaths to calm himself. He focused on a tiny chip in his desk. The crack, even though seemingly minuscule, ruined the perfection of the desk. Sometimes it's the small paper cuts that kill.

Alistair said goodbye to Bradley and they both hung up, downtrodden to say the least. Alistair gasped as an attempt to stop the tears from coming. Then in came Esme. She stopped at the doorway when she realized her father was crying hot tears.

"Why are you crying, Daddy?" She rushed to his side and hugged his arm. Alistair stood and hugged his daughter. She nestled her head into the crevice of his neck, and instantly a warming sensation ran down his spine. It reached out and grabbed the memories of the war and put them away for later. It heated up the cold and brought joy in each heartbeat. No matter the severity of the situation, Esme always cheered him up. He even found himself smiling.

"No reason, sweetie, no reason." Esme moved her head away from his shoulder and faced Alistair. She reached out with her small, precious hand and dried his tears. The sun began to shine on his face as his smile grew even more.

"Don't cry, Daddy." Alistair laughed and agreed not to. How could he be sad in the presence of an angel, his angel?

"I love you, Esme."

"Love you, Daddy. Horsey?" Alistair laughed again and put down Esme, got on all fours, and pretended to neigh. So long as he and the Snappy Kings were at peace, albeit shaky peace, he could have carefree moments with his daughter. Moments that strengthened his damaged roots of humanity. Moments that would forever shine in his memory. Moments that made him forget about the dire situation unfolding.

Almost.

CHAPTER 3

"Mr. Jameson, sir?" Alistair jumped awake. Mary had been shaking his shoulder gently, trying to wake him up. Alistair shook his head and ran his hand through his hair. He still donned the same clothes he wore yesterday, his black suit with a white tie, and he was still in his office.

"How long have I been sleeping, Mary?"

"I've been shaking you for about ten minutes. I reckon you need to go on holiday." Alistair put his hands up to stop Mary from talking. He couldn't fill his head with nonsense like time off from work. All his life, he'd never taken a holiday. To him, time away from work was torture. It emptied his mind of things to worry about and thus filled his mind with sharp memories of his past. No busy work meant his mind was working twice as hard to betray him, and nothing made him angrier than betrayal. Betrayal is reserved for cowards only. Cowards have no place in his heart, home, or organization. Cowards are the ultimate sinner, because it's basically suicide, at least to Alistair.

"Mary, can you please grab my pen?" Alistair pointed to his pen that lay across the room. He was unaware of how it got there.

"Sir, that one isn't going to work."

"Why not?" Alistair sighed, trying not to lose his patience. He already had a headache, and he rubbed his temples in an attempt to squander the discomfort in his brain. Mary looked down and smoothed out her black uniform.

"I don't know, sir. But last night you came out of your office demanding a new pen because you said yours wouldn't work anymore."

Alistair leaned forward on his desk and raised an eyebrow at Mary. "And why wouldn't it work, Mary?"

She shook her head and explained she didn't know. When she came in with another pen, he had passed out in his chair. She motioned at his desk, between where his hands lay.

"There's the new pen, sir." Alistair looked down, and sure enough, there was a pen right in front of him. He reached out and grabbed it.

"Mary, what was I doing last night?"

"I don't know, sir."

"Esme?"

"She's still sleeping. She came to say goodnight, but you were already asleep. She put a blanket on you and left, chanting, 'My daddy is having the sweetest of dreams!'" Alistair put his head down and smiled. As he did, he noticed a blanket that rested just in front of his feet. In typical Esme fashion, she didn't have a care in the world. She only saw the positive aspects of life. Even from the story Mary told him, Alistair felt the room get bright, so bright it hurt his head.

"That'll be all, Mary." She nodded and left. Alistair got up and walked across the room to his fallen pen. Mary was right, the pen's shell was completely broken. As he bent down to pick it up, his stomach flared and he got very dizzy. Sitting down, he rubbed his temples again. The light in the room penetrated his eyes and pierced his brain. The smells from the fresh bread being brought in from the bakery revolted him. He doubled over and breathed heavily. Then he turned his head and eyed the useless pen, a casualty of what Alistair could only assume was his anger. He grabbed it. The sharp craters in the shell were pierced, leaking ink all over his hands. He silently cursed and put the pen back down on the carpet, which was now stained with ink. He shakily climbed to his feet and walked across the hall to the bathroom. He turned the water on and let it clean his hands of the ink that dared to upset him. He looked at himself in the sink mirror and reacted unemotionally to how disheveled he appeared. He grabbed a fancy napkin and made his way back over to his desk. Last night he didn't work, and last night he was almost sure his mind betrayed him. He stared up in an attempt to show his mind his killer stare, the stare that could kill a lion with half a glance. He quickly looked down, however, as it hurt his eyes to look up. Mind over matter. Alistair rarely accepted defeat, but he realized he needed to now. He was smart; he knew to not pick battles with someone he couldn't beat.

Alistair reached out and grabbed a blank sheet of gold-tinted paper. He needed to get back to Alcott as soon as possible. Grabbing the new pen, but not forgetting the fallen one, he began to write.

Dear Mr. Alcott Dirkson,

The date is August 7th, 1930. How nice of you to reply in a timely fashion. I'm glad my letter brought joy to your dull heart. Hopefully the joy isn't lesser the second time.

Your condolences for my horse are all but arbitrary, Mr. Dirkson. Fake sympathy is hard to pass, and it will not be mistaken for anything sentimental. But don't worry, Mr. Dirkson. The second our exchanges stop, I'll get revenge. I know who did it, and I know you know too.

Let me be frank, Mr. Dirkson. I don't adhere to demands from men like you. And hear me when I say I'm not afraid of conflict with you. I never pick fights I can't win. Why would this be an exception?

Your memory is good, Mr. Dirkson. And I'm sorry you don't have any brothers or sisters; it's no wonder you turned out so characterless. Let's leave Davenport out of this; he's innocent.

Because your memory is so good, I'm sure you'll know

how the Brassy Gats have always enjoyed domination over the Snappy Kings. So let me ask you this, are you willing to spell disaster for your men and women? Because if so, allow me to don black in preparation for your funeral.

Don't order me around, Mr. Dirkson. Because even though my men have been told to stand down, I can easily change those orders.

Best regards,
Alistair Jameson,
Brassy Gats

Alistair rose and made his way out of his office. This was a letter he wanted to give to the mailman himself. He grabbed his hat and stuck it over his messy hair. As he descended down the stairs, he was met by Bradley, who looked equally disheveled and disoriented.

"You busy, brother?"

Alistair shook his head and turned back around into the office. Still, he needed this letter mailed within the hour. He checked his pocket watch: 07:30. Sensing Bradley's business here would exceed thirty minutes, he called out to Mary, who came around the corner. In her hand she had some fresh bread he'd smelled a couple minutes ago. Although this time, his stomach welcomed the smell of the bread and begged for it.

"Here, sir. Oh, Mr. Jameson! How rude of me. I didn't know you were coming. Allow me to grab you a plate." She rushed off and appeared with another plate and some marmalade.

"Thank you, Mary. I have another letter for you to send." Alistair extended his hand and Mary took the letter and left. Alistair then went into his office and closed the doors behind him. Bradley had already sat in a chair and was spreading the homemade marmalade over his warm bread. Alistair sat down next to his brother.

"What happened here?" Bradley nodded his head in the direction of the broken pen and the ink it had oozed onto the carpet.

"Why are you here, Brad?"

"You're dodging the question."

"I don't have time to talk about broken pens." But truthfully, Alistair rarely answered questions he didn't know the answer to. Only when it was absolutely necessary, and here this question was necessary to avoid.

Bradley sighed. "I came here to apologize."

"For what?"

"For bringing up the depressing day in France." Bradley's voice cracked. He was clearly sleep deprived and tired. Bradley usually had a lot of energy, but now he looked fragile. Alistair knew by the end of the day Bradley would perk up again, not necessarily by choice, but rather by necessity. And even though there were many sad days in France, Alistair knew exactly which one his brother was referring to. Alistair said nothing. He couldn't think of anything to say. He should've said, "It's all right," but those words scraped the back of his throat and he couldn't bear to talk about the subject further. Bradley cleared his throat and straightened up in his seat.

"And I came to talk about Wilcot Randy." Alistair shot his head forward, eyes directed right toward Bradley. Bradley now had his full attention.

"And?"

"And we've found no previous record of Randy ever being a butler." Alistair felt butterflies come to life as he feared the worst for Davenport.

"But he's not there to harm Davy. I talked to Father Romano yesterday and I told him about Wilcot. Father recognized the name instantly. He said Randy used to work for his church but left when he moved out to Conwy to pursue a fishing career. Father said Randy, like himself, is a pacifist, although Randy never served in the war because he's got asthma and high blood pressure."

"Oh, that's actually great." Alistair rose and grabbed a piece of bread from his desk. He felt his soul relax; his brother wasn't in harm's way.

"But there's one other thing. He's not a fisherman."

"Then what is he?"

"He's a psychologist." Alistair stopped chewing mid-bite. His soul moaned as it resumed its near constant tight position. His brother wasn't any safer in Conwy than he was in Burford.

"For crying out loud!" Alistair slammed his fist on his desk, knocking off a few papers.

"Ally, it's best not to confront Davy about this."

"Brad, the whole of our existence rests on Conwy. We can't have an unstable leader down there. But I can't send you down to replace him or he will lose his mind."

"Cut him some slack, Ally. Davy is resilient; he'll bounce right back."

"How'd he do it?"

"Excuse me?"

"How did he do it?" Alistair was angry. The whole of his operation was about to collapse on itself.

"He was drunk, Ally."

"How did he do it?" Alistair took two long strides and looked up, directly into Bradley's eyes with his killer stare. But his stare only worked on his enemies; his family was immune. Finally, Bradley sighed and rocked back and forth on his feet.

"He was drunk, Ally, and the rope snapped."

There was a knock at the door, and Alistair, still looking directly at Bradley, who by now had looked away, opened the door.

"Uncle Brad!" Esme came running in. Her skin neglected to sense the tension in the room as she ran right past Alistair and jumped into Bradley's arms. He scooped her up and put her on his shoulders. The room's overcast gray tone melted into a warm pink. The books, the papers, even the dead pen perked up to the sound of pure happiness. The room was at peace.

"Look, Daddy, I'm taller than you!" Esme squealed as Bradley glided across the room with Esme atop his shoulders.

"You sure are," Alistair laughed. Then Mary called out for Esme, saying she had a riding lesson. Esme shrieked with excitement. She loved nothing more than riding her palomino pony, Daffodil, that Alistair bought for her last year.

"Daddy, can you come with me?"

Alistair smiled gently at the memories of riding with his daughter. Sometimes they rode on his magnificent stallion, Atlas, together. Sometimes they rode side by side. And sometimes he'd watch his daughter in the paddock, jumping over the neatly placed hurdles. "I can't sweetie, I've got some things to take care of."

"Okay, Daddy. Bye, Uncle!" She waved and ran off to ride her pony.

Alistair chuckled softly and looked back at Bradley. "She's a cutie, isn't she?" Bradley nodded and agreed that she was his favorite niece, albeit his only niece.

"How's Loretta?"

"She's good, thanks." Bradley cleared his throat, reminding his brother of the situation at hand.

"Oh, right. Davy is lucky the rope snapped?"

"Yes."

"Well, given the doctor is there, there's no need for us to worry. Now, if you'll excuse me, I've got a meeting with Mr. Popov." Alistair went over to Bradley and slapped him on the back before reaching around him and grabbing the rest of his bread.

"Okay." Alistair turned and left the office with Bradley trailing behind him, still surprised by Alistair's change of heart. The two of them exited the warehouse and went their own directions. Alistair was rushing down the street to make it to the local pub for an important meeting with Andrei Popov. Part of him hated Popov, but he knew that a friendly relationship with Popov was invaluable, especially now with the threat of conflict looming over everyone. Alistair hastily made his way down the street. The farther Alistair got from home, the more the world turned gray. Young children played in the road, kicking a limp ball against a wall, yet somehow finding joy. Unlike happiness, joy cannot be faked. And joy doesn't knock when it wants to come in; joy lets itself in.

"Mr. Jameson?" Of course, ignorance can't last forever.

"Mr. Jameson!" Alistair stopped and realized he had walked

right past the pub where he needed to be. Specifically, he passed Andrei Popov.

"Mr. Popov." Alistair turned and walked back to the familiar pub. The two gentlemen, upon entering, quieted the whole place down. Alistair looked straight ahead as he swiftly passed the bar-goers. These were single men, willing to drink their money rather than save it. Alistair glided across the dusty wood floors and entered a small room on the far side. As soon as he and Andrei stepped inside, the chatter resumed.

"I thought you knew your way around town, Mr. Jameson." Andrei Popov's Russian accent was thick and salty. The accent struggled through the hardships of the war, although Popov had rarely seen the front lines. During the war, Popov enlisted as a doctor. He had trained in Russian medical schools before, but never trauma patients. Soon after, he was dishonorably discharged.

"I know my way around my city, Mr. Popov. I fought for it on the front lines." Alistair spoke with no change in tone. He wanted to remind Popov that two can play the Russian's guilt game.

"And I stole from your country to give to mine. I guess we're even then." This was why Alistair hated Popov. Popov smuggled Lee–Enfield rifles from the British and supplied them to the Russians on the front lines. The Lee–Enfield rifles were the best rifles the war produced, and Popov stole them. But it's also why Alistair needed Popov, because Popov could easily supply Alistair's men with better weapons than their enemy.

"Yes, and you were exiled." Alistair is one of very few people who knew where Popov was. He was exiled from Russia, and the Bolsheviks had been looking for him ever since. One tip-off from Alistair, and Popov would be dragged back to his homeland.

"Need we awaken old memories? Let's not wake those that need to sleep." His sharp Russian accent floated in the air.

"Mr. Popov, you don't like me anymore than I like you—"

"Nonsense, you and I are buddies."

"Are we?"

"Oh sure. And I'll tell you why. Today I was approached by a Mr. Oliver Eastaughffe regarding some weapons. Now, Mr.

Jameson, as I recall, I know you and Mr. Eastaughffe aren't friends like we are. I was honored, actually, because he told me that I was apparently the best weapons dealer in all of England. Can you imagine that? On this island, I am the best weapons dealer. You're lucky to have me."

"Mr. Popov, let's not digress."

"Perhaps you should treat me with a little more courtesy. Anyways, I told him he must have the wrong guy, as I am retired from weapons dealing. See, Mr. Jameson, I could've helped your enemy, but I didn't. That makes us buddies, doesn't it?"

"I need weapons, Mr. Popov."

"Really? I heard you and your enemies are at peace."

"I don't pay you to ask questions."

"All right, all right what do you need?"

"I want a hundred Winchester Model 54s."

"American hunting rifles?"

Alistair lifted his eyebrow and sighed. "Yes. And stored underneath I want a thousand and one Thompson submachine guns."

A quiet grin spread across Popov's face. "Now we're talking."

"How much will that cost?"

"You want a thousand and one, very odd number if I do say so myself, Thompson submachine guns. So if each one is fifteen hundred pounds, that's 1.5 million pounds—"

"I won't be paying that much, Mr. Popov. So either you take this deal for three hundred thousand pounds or I'll report you to the Russians."

"Let's not make haste—"

"I don't like my time to be wasted. Three hundred thousand pounds or the deal is off and you go back to Russia." Alistair extended his hand forward, waiting for Popov to shake it. Reluctantly, Popov accepted defeat and reached his hand out. The two embraced in a physical contract.

"Here's twenty thousand pounds now. I'll give you the rest when I see my American guns." Alistair reached into his deep trench coat pocket and pulled out a wad of cash. Alistair never carried more than twenty thousand pounds at a time. It was too risky, even for a man of his status. When the poor are desperate for survival, nobody is safe. And unfortunately, nearly everyone he saw nowadays was poor. There was little escape from the pandemic of poverty. Alistair, however, was immune.

"Pleasure doing business with you, Mr. Popov." Alistair turned and walked to the doorway.

"The pleasure's all mine, Mr. Jameson." Alistair hesitated before he opened the door and walked toward the pub exit. Once again, his presence brought an unnatural silence. Only after he left did the music and drunken mumbling continue. Alistair took a deep breath and walked, head up, to his stables. If he hurried, he could still see his daughter's riding lesson. Maybe he could do some riding of his own. But of course, that was a fantasy. And of course there was always something still to be done.

"Mr. Jameson!" Alistair looked around, but he couldn't see anyone.

"Mr. Jameson!" Alistair spun around. There was Andrei Popov.

"Mr. Popov?" Alistair noticed a clear change in Popov's demeanor. The normally calm Popov had switched into a tight one. His words slurred into a jumble of nonsense. He reached out and put his hand on Mr. Jameson to steady himself. For a man who had to walk not ten steps, he was out of breath. Alistair began to get concerned.

"Mr. Jameson. You and I may not always see eye to eye, but you know that I don't like innocent deaths. I was sitting at the bar waiting to get some vodka, and I heard three men speaking Russian. I'll spare you the details, but they said that they hated you. They said you led the city to poverty. Clearly they are mistaken, but they said they needed money and they had a plan to get it. Mr. Jameson, your daughter isn't safe. They said they've been following her and your maid every day, and they know exactly when and where to get her." Alistair snapped his neck up. He stormed right past Popov and burst through the bar, breaking the door down. There was no way he'd let someone get away with even thinking about harming his daughter. He was livid, fueled by a fatherly protection.

"Which ones are they?" Alistair looked over his shoulder and noticed Mr. Popov wasn't there.

"Andrei!" Alistair shouted so loud the bartender dropped his bottle of expensive-looking whiskey. Popov came running and leaped into the bar.

"Who are they?" Alistair demanded answers. He needed to protect the purest human he knew. There was nothing he wouldn't do for Esme. Popov pointed to three men who sat around a round table in the back. Alistair followed Popov's finger. He menacingly walked toward the table. Once he reached it, he slammed his hands down on the table.

"Hello, gentlemen. I'm sure you know who I am. Forgive me, as I don't know your names." The men glanced at each other. They all bore scars on their faces, and Alistair knew they weren't from the war. They were fighting scars.

"Dammit! Tell me, is my daughter safe?" Alistair was screaming. He knew the whole street could hear, and he was glad. Let everyone take witness of the atrocity the three men were planning. Alistair thought he heard Bradley shout his name, but his mind could've been playing tricks on him. The mind likes to play games on the soul. At that moment, the church bells rang, shoving their noise into the faces of everyone in the pub. The three gentlemen looked at each other, then at Alistair, and smiled.

"You hear that, Mr. Jameson? The clock strikes nine. Do you know what that means?"

"It means you'll get the hell out of my city and go as far away from my daughter as hell is to her."

"No," the lead man chuckled slyly, "it means you're too late. Hold on to the memories, Mr. Jameson. They'll soon be all you have left." Alistair grabbed the man's whiskey glass and shattered it over the man's face. Then he turned and ran out of the pub, sprinting to the stables. His heart froze from the fear of outliving his daughter, all the while simultaneously beating to the rhythm his soul danced to. *Esme, pulse, Esme, pulse, Esme.*

CHAPTER 4

Alistair ran. He ran down the barren streets, clear of all humanity. There was an unsettling calm that Alistair might've otherwise noticed, but he was hyperfocused on his daughter. There was no doubt in his mind she was in danger; after all, he knew Popov wouldn't dare lie. The soles of his shoes began to tear from the intensity of his desperation. The wind rushed around his face and gushed into his throat, dragging with it the tension of nothingness. His hat had long ago abandoned his head, and the air grasped at his hair in an attempt to slow him. His lungs burned, yet continued to do what was asked of them. But most of all, his heart cried and ached with each breath. There was little Alistair could do to calm his mind as it concocted its own tragedy titled, *Esme.* But still Alistair ran. And still Alistair ran into no one; only one car passed him, and he barely noticed. He tasted dust in his mouth from the wheels. He arrived, finally, to the open fields of his stables. He attempted to rush through the golden gates, but the second he did, he felt a prick in the back of his neck. He instinctively tried to flick it off, but it wouldn't budge. Whipping his head around, but still running, he tried to dislodge what he could only assume was a stubborn bug. But suddenly his legs went limp and he crashed onto the ground, unable to brace himself with his arms. His face struck the dirt, and the only thing he could move was his eyes. Pebbles cut his face, and the dust from the unpaved road floated freely into his airways. He tried to cough it up, but he found even that movement hard.

"Mr. Jameson!" Alistair knew that voice very well. And he now hated that voice. "Mr. Jameson! Oh, how rude am I? You can't move, can you?" All Alistair could let out was a grunt. He had been betrayed. He was now in the presence of a coward.

"Take him away." Alistair was suddenly picked up. He swayed back and forth in the brute's arms like a rag doll. Each limb lay in the hands of nature, as it moved with the wind and fell with it.

"Your daughter is unharmed, Mr. Jameson. It was never about Esme." Alistair rolled his eyes as he was quickly and quietly thrown into a car. He couldn't tell for sure, but he was almost certain this was the car that had passed him in his mad dash to save his daughter. As the car ignition turned on, Alistair felt the rumble of the motor in his stomach. It traveled upward and into his brain, which bobbled with each rock the car drove over. Alistair grunted in protest, but to no avail.

"Calm down, Mr. Jameson, it's only temporary. To be honest, I'm not sure how you're still awake." Alistair thrashed his tongue but couldn't make a sound. He fought and fought to keep his eyes open, but the more the car bounced on the unpaved road, the more his body jerked, and the more the darkness tugged away at his light, he found it hard. Finally, he couldn't do it anymore. He closed his eyes, and the absence of light brought forth the absence of consciousness.

"Lieutenant!" Alistair risked a quick glance to his left from his position. The chaos of war around him mixed with the cries made it hard for him to hear his comrades.

"Lieutenant!" He heard it again. Somewhere, farther along from his position, someone was calling for him. He turned to his partner, Racin' Ricky, and nodded. Ricky nodded back and took a step away from the top of the trench and into the precarious safety below. Alistair sprinted, head down and low to the ground, to the next post. There was only one man controlling two machine guns. Alistair looked down and noticed one of his own rolling around in agony. Alistair knelt down and grabbed his hand.

"You're all right. Where'd it hit you?" The soldier pointed to his lower right abdomen and cried with each short inhale. Alistair cradled the soldier's head.

"Medic! Medic!" Alistair watched as Father Romano emerged from underground. When he reached them, he knelt and gently stroked the wounded man's head too.

"God is on your side. God knows you've done a great deal for your country, and thus his. Shhh, our Lord has plans for you, young man. Calm, breathe. The pain you feel is only temporary. Let the light of Jesus Christ shine brightly in your dim soul. Focus on the clouds above; our savior is in the clouds above, watching. Shhh, they'll save you, soldier." Father Romano was much better at comforting the wounded than Alistair. Alistair also felt relieved; if the Father said that the wounded man would be saved, then the wound sustained wasn't fatal.

"Lieutenant!" Alistair slowly rose and turned to search for whomever was calling now. He knew that this soldier would live, and he considered that to be a miracle. But suddenly, everything came crashing down—or, rather, up. A massive explosion rocked the trenches. Alistair was flung out of the trench and into the open field. He was thankful he wasn't flung into no-man's-land, or he'd surely be dead. But then his heart froze. His brain cried and wept as he noticed two of the most important people in his life scrambling to get out of no-man's-land. He lurched forward, ignoring the blood that raced down his leg. He didn't care about a cut from shrapnel. But it didn't matter; he'd never make it in time to save them. He watched helplessly as time stood still. Bullets fell woefully short of him as he had been thrown in the opposite direction of no-man's-land. He couldn't think about the cries of the wounded and the silence of the dead; he could only focus on the men caught in no-man's-land. He felt tears gush from his eyes and crash hard into the depressed ground. He felt his heartbeat quicken to an uncontrollable pace and his lungs shake with each painful breath. Suddenly, he saw Davenport dash out from the trenches and tackle one of the men caught in no-man's-land. The bullets just nicked the savior's back instead of tearing through the heart of the intended victim. But there was only one savior and two men. Alistair felt his mouth open wide and shout, but he couldn't hear anything. The world had gone silent and he heard only the impacts of one, two, three, four, five bullets tear through the weak flesh and penetrate deep into the exposed body.

"No!" Alistair's vision was blurred. He had never felt such grief before. He heard echoes of the word *no*. The entire platoon had stopped and turned to Alistair, who now was raw with emotion. Pure rage and grief flooded his body. His nerves quivered, and his soul sank. Running pointlessly, he collapsed. His brain thundered against his skull, and his eyes threatened to pop out. But it didn't matter anymore; the damage had already been done.

"Mr. Jameson!" A man who Alistair only assumed was the Father was shaking him. He whipped his hand around in an attempt to get the man to stop. He wanted the world to see the grief. He wanted to melt and fly away with the soul he just witnessed go.

"Mr. Jameson!" The shaking only got harder.

"Mr. Jameson!"

Alistair's eyes sprung open. He hopped up from the floor, heart beating, and looked around.

"He's awake, the drugs wore off." It took a moment for Alistair's eyes to adjust to the dim room. He felt sweat drip from his forehead and land softly on the ground below. He wasn't sure where he was, but from what he could see, it looked like a shed in the middle of nowhere. There were no windows, and only two lights lit the room enough for Alistair to see the amount of trouble he was in. Specifically, he was able to see the barrel of a gun pointed right at his head.

"Sit, Mr. Jameson, stay a while."

"I'll stand."

"Setting terms? Mr. Jameson, I didn't have to be kind enough to not only drag you here in one piece, but I only gave you temporary drugs. Please do be grateful, my friend."

"We aren't buddies anymore."

"Sure we are. Although my gun aimed right at your head might put a damper in our relationship."

Alistair couldn't take it anymore. "What do you want, Mr. Popov?"

"What do I want? Ha!" Popov looked around the room, chuckling, "Mr. Jameson, I want my money. I want two million or else you're dead. That doesn't seem unreasonable, does it, gentlemen?" The three men from the bar circled around Popov nodded in agreement. Monotone chirps of "No, sir" floated pathetically in the air.

"Let me tell you something, Mr. Jameson. The peasants in your town, your Burford, all respect you. Granted, they don't have much of a choice, but they respect you. But if respect is the only thing protecting you from a knife in the back, respect means nothing, right?"

"Let me tell you something, Mr. Popov. I learned this, clearly, the hard way."

"Oh, do be quick with it, Mr. Jameson. This gun isn't going to fire itself."

"Sometimes the person who you'd take a bullet for is the one with their finger on the trigger."

"I'm flattered, really. But flattery is pretty worthless, and I need money. So, what will it be?"

"My offer made back at the pub was final."

"Are you sure about that?"

"Absolutely. Remember, when you kill me, you'll have the Brassy Gats to deal with."

"You think that scares me? I've been hiding from the Bolsheviks for ten years."

"You can't hide forever, Mr. Popov. Even the ghosts come out."

Alistair looked Popov square in the eye. He saw Popov try not to squirm, but he was no match for Alistair's stare.

"Enough! Mr. Jameson, I have the gun, do I not?"

"That's correct."

"Then I have the power."

Alistair grinned and chuckled. "Mr. Popov, you're shallow if you think guns make you powerful. It's respect. Respect isn't meaningless, as you have so suggested."

"I'm getting tired, Mr. Jameson. Believe me, I'd love to continue this conversation, but I must put a bullet in your head now. You understand, don't you?" Alistair heard the gun click as Popov cocked his weapon. For the first time, Alistair felt fear. He took two paces backward, but he was still in point-blank range, so it didn't matter. Once again, all he could think about was Esme. How was she going to feel if she grew up an orphan? And the fallen soldier. Esme and the fallen. *Old soldiers never die.*

"Sorry, Mr. Jameson."

Bang! Alistair looked across the horizon. He knew the enemy knew they were coming, and now he heard the Germans' gunfire, even though he couldn't see them. Surely that meant the Germans could hear him too.

"Ally." Bradley came jogging up next to him. Alistair looked at his brother and offered an unconvincing smile. Bradley met his smile before stumbling and grabbing his leg. This was the beginning of Bradley's permanent leg injury.

"The leg?" Bradley nodded. Alistair sighed and let his brother lean on him. No one in the platoon had high spirits. Everyone knew that the plan to drive the Germans back was going to fail. Already aspects of the higher command's master plan began to collapse on itself. And to make matters worse, none of the brothers knew if Davenport was all right. But they were, in a backward way, excited to reach their destination because it meant they could rejoice in their little brother's company once more.

"I can't wait to see Davy." The brothers nodded in agreement. They all missed Davenport. Of course, they were content being alone and safe because the closer and closer they got to Davenport, the closer they got to the unavoidable fate: death. Be it theirs or be it someone else's, death is always guaranteed in war. Alistair turned around and studied his men. He was in charge of this platoon, he was in charge of the mighty force behind him. He wished the Germans would give up; everyone hated them already, so why fear being the coward? He just wanted to go home, to relax with his wife. He just wanted to live a normal life. He just wanted to enjoy his brothers' company without the fear of being killed. The bare necessities of life were stripped away from every soldier no matter the country. In a way, the Great War united the soldiers bearing the brunt of their countries' stupidity. *Bang!* Alistair didn't even flinch. *Bang! Bang! Bang!*

Bang! Alistair's mind sprung awake. In front of him lay Popov and his three men, all dead. And there in the doorway stood Davenport, gun still smoking. Alistair looked down to the dead and back to Davenport, mouth wide open in shock.

"How—?"

"I was almost too late."

"How did you know, Davy?"

"About five days ago I saw Popov in Conwy. Guess I won't be seeing him around anymore. Anyways, he was acting very suspicious and I followed him. He turned down the Snappy Kings' side street and wasn't fired at. I knew then that meant he'd done a deal with the Snappy Kings. Then three days ago, I saw him again, this time speaking Russian. I could only understand a little bit, so I called Lev, my Russian friend, to invite Mr. Popov for drinks, Russian to Russian. Anyways, two days ago Lev flew in and got Popov talking. Popov revealed his 'plans to murder a big gang boss.' Lev told me this morning, and I came speeding down to the location Popov gave Lev. Clearly Popov isn't smart. I did him a favor by blowing his brains out. I tried to warn you, remember? Oh, and I phoned Bradley, he's on the way." Davenport spat on Popov's fresh corpse. Alistair smiled.

"You saved my life, Davy." Alistair saw Davenport light up with joy. There was nothing Davenport loved more than being the savior. Alistair stepped around the dead, and together, arm in arm, the two brothers left the shed. Alistair was indeed right, they were in the middle of nowhere. He looked his brother up and down. Davenport was shorter than Alistair, and he was convinced that's why Davenport was sent underground. But what his younger brother lacked in size, he made up for in strength. Davenport was one of the strongest men Alistair knew, and Alistair met a lot of men every day. Davenport was also feared more than Alistair, mainly because Davenport's first instinct was shoot first, ask later. It certainly saved Alistair's life, but it also proved dangerous. Davenport wasn't mature enough, nor could he ever be, to realize violence will only go half way. Alistair realized that long ago.

"Davy?"

"Yeah?" Davenport turned his head and faced his brother. Alistair had so many things to say, but he couldn't pick just one. Davenport needed to hear the wise words of an elder, words even Alistair lacked. Alistair sighed. He put his hand on Davenport's back.

"Thank you." Alistair instantly flinched. That wasn't what he wanted to say. His brain shoved those words straight into his mouth.

"Don't mention it." Davenport looked at his brother and offered a half smile. Alistair met his smile before signaling to a fallen tree trunk. The two brothers went over and sat on the log.

"The forest is beautiful, eh?"

"Yes. All is calm." Alistair nodded and looked around. Had it not been for the near death experience, he would've had a lovely time. All the Jameson brothers found a sense of peace in the woods. For Alistair, it was the gentle breeze that cleansed the soul and the damp moss that squished between his toes. The forest was his home away from home. But his eyes soon settled on the shed. It broke the spell of the woods. Alistair put his hands on his thighs and leaned forward, clearing his throat.

"You know how he got me?" Davenport shook his head no. Alistair rose gently and placed his foot on the log. "He tricked me, then he drugged me. But when I was out cold from the drugs, my mind wanted to inflict more pain than Popov. My bloody mind spat out a bad memory, *the* bad memory." Alistair saw Davenport recoil in pain. The mental strain the weight of this memory carried was giving all the brothers back pain.

"We don't talk about that, Alistair." Alistair expected this. He knew there was little he could do to get Davenport to open up. But he knew if he wanted to rid Davenport of this leech, he had to let it draw blood first.

"Davy, listen to me. He's not dead to us. If you don't talk about him, then he'll surely die."

"I killed him!" Davenport shot up like a rocket, tears drowning his weakened flesh.

"No! You didn't kill him, you saved Bradley."

"I had to pick! I couldn't even see clearly, my eyes were already damaged from the explosion. I went for who was closer. I went for who was closer." Davenport wobbled on his feet. The tears kept flowing, and they wouldn't stop. Alistair knew this was best for Davenport.

"I was so scared I'd lose them both. My tunneling journeys paled in comparison to that moment. I had life and death in my hands, and I could only save one. I could only save one!" Davenport collapsed into Alistair's arms. He put his hands up and wailed, a cry so heart-wrenching, it brought Alistair to tears. Alistair fell to his knees and together they wept. The sadness only humanity could experience bent the leaves, the clouds, and the gentle breeze. Everything that witnessed the woeful sight joined in the mourning. The whole world shrank to grief. No joy dared shine through in a place where agony demanded space. The despair grabbed the sun and threw it far away. It sheltered the anguish from the light, calling in all the clouds far and wide.

It showed no signs of stopping. Then, coming around the bend, footsteps. Hurried footsteps, as their owner was well aware of the tragic atmosphere. Alistair saw Bradley come into view. Davenport noticed him, too, and the second he did, Davenport rushed and hugged his brother.

"I could only save one." Davenport's misery threatened to hold his mouth shut. Alistair sniffled, cleared his throat, and stood.

"When the dam breaks, water comes gushing out." Alistair walked forward and stroked Davenport on the back. Bradley looked shocked, but he never let go of Davenport. Alistair saw Bradley's eyes tear up, and he knew Bradley had been infected with the disease of sorrow.

"It's all right, Davy. You saved me. Without you, I wouldn't be here." Alistair watched all of Davenport's body tense and teeth grind. Alistair winced; he never expected this from Davenport. But Alistair wasn't concerned; wounds heal twice as strong.

"Old soldiers never die, you remember?"

Davenport sniffled and looked at Alistair. "How could I forget?" he choked.

"Then as long as we're alive, he'll be alive," Bradley chimed in. Alistair glanced at Bradley and shared a knowing glance. Alistair could sense Bradley was ready to explode with grief, but they both had to be strong for Davenport's sake.

"Old soldiers never die," Davenport weakly repeated.

"Old soldiers never die."

"Old soldiers never die."

CHAPTER 5

August 9, 1930

Dear Mr. Alistair Jameson,

I write this letter with no intention of ever receiving a reply. You fell for the trap of peace, Mr. Jameson. Now I can don black for your funeral, and the funeral for your scrappy Brassy Gats. It's fun, really, having total control of the exportation of gin. Who knew it would be this simple?

I'll keep this letter brief, because it's just not the same writing to a deceased man. Unrewarding, to say the least. Conwy will fall to me, as Davenport will surely be too distraught to lead a defense in Conwy. Should I tell you my plan? Might as well, so students can study my brilliance.

The plan is simple: win. Good day to you in hell, Mr. Jameson.

Best Regards,
Alcott Dirkson,
Snappy Kings

Alistair furrowed his brow. Not only had Dirkson planned the events of yesterday, but he had broken the unspoken promise of peace, and that left Alistair with no time to get weapons from America; he had to fight with what he already had.

"Ally?" Alistair looked up. Davenport came waltzing in, an unusual ease floating around him. Alistair had gotten used to the gray cloud that went everywhere with his brother, and it was refreshing to see Davenport happy, or at least not totally sad.

"What's on your wrist?" Alistair pointed to a pink piece of paper on Davenport's arm. Davenport laughed. Alistair rose from his seat, dumbfounded. He couldn't remember the last time he'd heard his brother laugh.

"Esme made it for me. She was playing princess alone, so I joined her. She cut out a pink heart and placed it on my arm so I could be a princess too." Davenport glowed. His brother was happy, and Alistair couldn't believe it. Something must've happened, something good.

"Anyways, I came here to tell you something." Davenport's joy still stood strong. "My wife, Cordelia, phoned me this morning. She's pregnant, Ally, I'm going to be a father." Alistair didn't know what to say. His brother, his immature and unstable brother, was going to have a child of his own. He didn't think Davenport was ready—even Bradley had no children. But that didn't matter, because Alistair saw how happy the news made his brother. Although Davenport wasn't totally smiling, he could sense his brother's heart was.

"Congratulations, Davy." Alistair grabbed his brother's hand and pulled him into a hug. Alistair could feel Davenport's heart dancing, bringing a new energy to the room. Alistair's doubts melted away as he felt Davenport's energy.

"I have to go tell Brad now. I can't believe this, I really can't. I think that, for the first time in a long time, I'm looking forward to something." Davenport turned and walked out of Alistair's office with a newfound pep in his step. This couldn't have been any more different from the Davenport he saw last night, the one whose breaths were scarred with sadness. This Davenport glowed. He knew not which Davenport to trust, but he liked Davenport better with some elation. He didn't have the heart to tell Davenport that Conwy was in immediate danger. He'd have to tell Bradley first.

"Daddy! Daddy!" Esme came running into his office.

"My beautiful Esme. What can I do for you?" Esme jumped into his arms and he scooped her up and put her on his shoulders.

"Nothing, Daddy, I just wanted to say hello." Alistair smiled and gently let his daughter down. She scurried off, leaving a trail of purity behind her. Alistair chuckled to himself and shook his head in disbelief. He still couldn't believe his youngest brother was going to be a father. Again, he couldn't worry about Davenport, but he could indeed feel delighted for him. Just then, the phone rang, and Alistair looked up in surprise, not expecting a phone call from anyone.

"Hello?"

"Alistair, thank goodness."

"Father Romano, is everything all right?"

"It is now. Word on the street is you're dead." The Father sounded anxious, and that shocked Alistair. Father Romano was never worried; he always was confident God would protect him and his loved ones, Alistair included. But he was worried about Alistair.

"No, Father, I'm alive." Alistair chuckled. There was an odd peace deep in his body; the weight of life disappeared with the lightness of death. But Alistair's body felt too light; he needed the weight to keep him grounded. Humanity needed the hardships of life to ground their roots. Humanity is shaped by those hardships.

"Alistair, what does this mean?"

"War, Father, war." Father Romano shuddered. The mention of war sent chills down the veterans' backs, down the widows' hearts, and through the Jameson brothers' souls. After a while, the Father broke his silence.

"Greater love has no one than this: to lay down one's life for one's friends."

"Old soldiers never die."

"Yes, old soldiers never die."

"Do you think about him?"

"I dwell not on the dead; I cherish the dying."

"I think about him every day. If I didn't—"

"Hush this nonsense, Alistair."

"Davenport blames himself."

"Davenport could only save one."

Alistair checked his watch, forcing back the memories sneaking forward. He heard the Father ramble on about God, but he wasn't listening. He needed to find a way to save Conwy, and he had to make that his main priority. After all, if his mind was busy, his heart wouldn't break. The line was silent. Alistair had been so consumed in his own affairs, he hadn't realized Father Romano had hung up. Angrily, he tossed the receiver back on the cradle. He didn't know why he was angry, nor who—or what, for that matter—his anger was channeled at. Perhaps he was angry about the barbarians that forever changed the course of his life, or perhaps he was angry at the angels who failed to keep the barbarians away from his life. Whatever the case, he was angry. He threw his head back and let out a yell deep from within the folds of his chest, a much-needed cleaning of the cobwebs growing in his body. He felt feelings long hidden in his chest come pouring out in a single yell. He took a deep breath and forced the straggling feelings back to their malnourished homes. He closed his eyes and let the air around his head float gently into his ears. Davenport's pure joy in his right ear calmed his soul, while Davenport's misery in his left ear blocked the sound of life. Humanity and nature clashed in his brain in an attempt to take control over his thoughts. This was a battle that had no winner.

"Mr. Jameson, sir?"

"Yes, Mary?" For once in Alistair's life, Mary's presence annoyed him. He just wanted to be left alone. Whether she heard his upset tone or chose to ignore it, Alistair didn't know.

"Sir, Mr. Bradley Jameson has requested a family meeting downstairs." Alistair groaned and rose from his chair. Most of his working life had been spent in his office, and leaving it felt like leaving his kingdom. He followed Mary out and shut his door. He made his way down the spiral staircase onto the ground level. Everyone in the room stopped what they were doing and looked at Alistair. Echoes of "Hello, Mr. Jameson" spread like wildfire. He walked straight down the middle of all the calm chaos. He felt powerful. He felt like his platoon marched with him. He felt the hands of the fallen on his back as they walked beside him. Finally, and unfortunately for Alistair, he reached the grand meeting room. In front of the doors stood Davenport and Bradley.

"Some entrance, Ally," Bradley joked and slapped his brother on the shoulder. The wooden doors shut with a loud bang.

"What's wrong, Brad?"

"We need to talk strategy." Bradley put his knuckles on the table and scratched his head. "We need to find a way to mobilize a fighting force in Conwy." This was the reason Alistair made Bradley his right-hand man. He had a strong head atop strong shoulders, and where Davenport lacked intelligence, Bradley lacked muscle. He certainly wasn't weak, but he was no match for Davenport's strength. Just as Davenport's intellect was no match for Bradley's.

"Strategy for what?" Davenport asked.

"Fighting, Davy. War." Alistair saw Davenport's unusual calm recede, and an expected anger began making its way to the front.

"You said they promised peace."

"Dirkson was behind my death."

Davenport started pacing around the room, although he remained relatively composed. "You're alive." The amount of anxiety in Davenport's speech was so glaring, even Alistair began to worry. But he knew that there was no way to reconcile with the Snappy Kings; war had to come.

"Ally's not alive to the Snappy Kings, Davy. To them he is dead." Bradley remained calm and composed, but that was nothing new. Bradley was almost always nonchalant.

"Exactly, which means to him we are weak and easy to prey upon." Davenport still seemed startled.

"Davy, we need you to move Cordelia out of Conwy. Bring her here—"

"You're insane. No! There can be another way, there's always another way!" Davenport began to get restless. Alistair understood, but if Cordelia was his wife, he would've moved her out long ago.

"Think about your unborn child, Davy." Bradley walked over to Davenport's side and put his hand on Davenport's shoulder. "You don't want them killed, do you?" Alistair both heard and saw something snap in Davenport, who whipped his arm around and struck Bradley square in the face. Bradley, taken by surprise, fell backward. Yet still, Bradley stood up, unconcerned. He kept his hands by his sides and casually pulled a chair away from the table and sat down.

"Davenport!" Alistair, on the other hand, was totally shocked. He knew his brother could be violent at times, but he expected Davenport to keep himself controlled around his family.

"Are you going to hit your wife when she disagrees with you too? Are you going to strike your child when they need help? Pull yourself together!" Alistair found himself responding equally immaturely to Davenport's immature notions. Davenport jumped, width wise, over the long table and landed inches from Alistair's face. Alistair never flinched.

"I'm a great husband, and I'm going to be a great father!"

"Then prove it."

Davenport stomped his leg. It was clear to Alistair that Davenport wanted to beat him. But in Alistair's eyes there was no better way to force Davenport to grow than by exposing his flaws.

"Prove it? Prove it? I proved it on the battlefield! I have two gallantry medals—not you, not Bradley, me!"

"Congratulations, soldier. You were always a soldier, Davenport. I was a lieutenant, so I know strategy. Now sit down and listen."

"Don't tell me what to do!"

"Davy, he's right. Davy, you have estimable qualities, immeasurable strength, and undying loyalty. You're like a young lion—"

"More matter with less art," Davenport responded dryly. Alistair and Bradley exchanged a quick, shocked glance.

"You read Shakespeare?" Alistair couldn't believe it. Nothing about his youngest brother fit the profile of an avid reader. Davenport was impulsive, but reading was slow and deliberate, especially Shakespeare.

"All the world's a stage, and all the men and women merely players. They have their exits and their entrances; and one man in his time plays many parts." Alistair felt his jaw drop off. Here was yet another Davenport; this Davenport was no fool. This Davenport wasn't the same Davenport that lashed out at Bradley not two minutes ago.

"The fool doth think he is wise, but the wise man knows himself to be a fool." Davenport slowly walked back around to the other side of the table and sat down. Bradley cleared his throat, and Alistair, still astonished, took a seat.

"Strategy." Bradley cleared his throat again, still unable to move on from Davenport's reciting Shakespeare. "I propose we send back one of Ally's consultants to lead the war efforts in Conwy. That way, the Snappy Kings will believe they've forced our whole organization to implode."

"I'll bring Cordelia out here. You're right, she can't be in that kind of danger." Alistair nodded happily, as his brother was coming around. Yet something still didn't sit right with Alistair.

"We should send Davy back. If he can act like I was just killed, Dirkson will believe we are weaker. Even though Popov and his men won't report back to Dirkson, Dirkson knows Popov. He'll think he went back into hiding."

"Are you sure about that, Ally? You just witnessed my anger."

"Yes, Davy. I may have just seen how impulsive you are, but I also saw how wise you are. I've underestimated you." Davenport looked surprised, but it didn't match Alistair's shock. He still couldn't get over the Davenport he just saw for the first time.

"And I also propose, Bradley, that you gather your own fighting force and pretend like you want total control and that you're willing to fight Davy for it. Maybe even try to do a deal with the Snappy Kings."

"I see what you mean. I'll get in touch with Dirkson right away."

"Are you sure he won't see through your plan, Ally?"

"No, but risks are needed for success." Alistair looked at his hands. Davenport raised a good point; should Dirkson find out Alistair is still alive, he'd slaughter Bradley and his troops. But he was gravely outgunned, as the guns from America were never coming. He needed a quick victory and an unorthodox method.

"Brad, what do you think?" Bradley hesitated for a moment, probably running every scenario through his head.

"If the plan fails, it's going to fail to the uttermost degree. But if it succeeds, it's going to succeed spectacularly." Bradley turned to face Davenport. "There is a tide in the affairs of men, which, taken at the flood, leads on to fortune—"

"Omitted, all the voyage of their life is bound in shallows and in miseries." Davenport smiled. There it was, a genuine Davenport smile. Alistair knew that smile wouldn't last, but in the moment, the smile held more power than Alistair's stare. The weak are only strong according to the definition of the strong, not the weak's own notions. In a natural world, there are no weak and no strong, there is only the weaker and the stronger.

"Then it is settled. Davy will lead the men in Conwy and Brad will sabotage the Snappy Kings." Alistair extended his hand to Bradley, who shook his hand, then to Davenport. That sealed it; their emergency plan had been formulated.

"How quickly can you two gather men?"

"I've already got men. The group from the north watch arrived yesterday," Bradley responded.

"I can have a small force put together by tonight," Davenport said.

"Excellent." Alistair began to stand but stopped when he noticed Davenport was signaling to stay seated.

"I have something to say. Cordelia and I came to an agreement the day she realized she was expecting my child. She wants to give the baby a name if it is a girl, and I will name it if it is a boy."

"Congratulations, Davy." Bradley slapped his brother on the shoulder and chuckled.

"Thanks, Brad. We've already picked out the names."

"That's great, Davy." Alistair was getting a little impatient. He didn't understand the reason he was still here, as he had some behind-the-scenes warfare to get to. Davenport sighed, clearly a bit upset with all the interruptions.

"If it is a girl, she wants to name her Harriet. And if it is a boy, which I am hoping for—"

"Daughters are great, too, Davy. I love my Esme."

"Let me finish."

"Sorry."

"And if it's a boy, I'm naming him Colburn." The mention of the name Colburn shot around the space like a dagger. It set fire to the brothers' hearts and sucked the name back into their vocabularies. There wasn't much Alistair could do to resist the pain that name dealt, but he welcomed it. It was a harsh slap in the face, and sometimes that is exactly what one needs. There was both a sharp pain and a calm relief. The pressure on his soul slowly fizzed out, and he didn't know what was happening. The name, which had been the source of his infection, was helping him begin to heal. For a long time, others' attempts to restore balance in Alistair fell on deaf ears and a dead soul. Mostly because he rejected help, he never wanted to hear that name again. But it felt good, it was refreshing. In a mere seven letters, he felt his soul rejuvenate and rejoice in a feeling of eternal happiness. The piece that the war took was gently placed, albeit cracked and unwhole, back in its place, a place where it should've been long ago. He should cherish the name more, not flat-out refuse it. A name was an understatement, because behind every name is a life. Behind that name was a hole where life should've been. And just the mere mention of it breathed some life back into it. It was a name that should've long ago been spoken about, a name that should've been surrounded with love not despair. It was a name Alistair never could, nor wanted to, forget.

Colburn.

CHAPTER 6

"Colburn?" Alistair checked his clock. It read midnight, way too late for Colburn to be awake. Alistair grunted as he drowsily reached out and lit a candle. The six-year-old with auburn red hair stood, holding his light-blue blanket close to his chest. He was only three years younger than Alistair, but he looked so much younger than that.

"Ally, Ally, I had a bad dream."

Alistair sat up in his bed and signaled for Colburn to sit next to him. A little smile spread across the boy's face as he jumped into Alistair's bed.

"It's all right, Colburn. Do you want me to read you a story?" Colburn vigorously nodded his small head yes. Alistair quietly laughed and tiptoed out of bed and to the bookshelf. He didn't have many stories to read. His parents loved poetry, and they filled his shelf with books upon books of poems.

"Okay, Colburn. Here's one of your favorite poems." Alistair turned and walked, slowly, so as to not make a sound, back to his bed, where Colburn waited eagerly. He clapped his hands and bounced. Alistair smiled, and his heart filled with joy; after all, he was practically raising Colburn.

"The Frost performs its secret ministry, unhelped by any wind. The owlet's cry came loud—and hark, again! Loud as before." Alistair continued reading the poem, and beside him, Colburn pretended to be an owl. He *whoo*ed silently and flapped his wings. Colburn loved owls, and he always tried to get his head to rotate all the way around. Alistair couldn't help but laugh. Colburn still had a firm grasp on his innocence. Soon, Alistair realized Colburn had stopped moving. He rolled his eyes, laughing, and pulled the blanket over Colburn. Rising, Alistair made his way to Colburn's room. He didn't want his parents to hear him, nor did he want to wake the sleeping Colburn.

"Alistair! What are you doing?" He knew that thunderous voice belonged to his father. "Colburn better not be in your room."

"No," Alistair lied. His parents didn't understand that Colburn had an abnormal amount of nightmares.

"Alistair!"

Alistair backed away from his aggravated father.

"Alistair!"

"Alistair!"

Alistair jumped awake. In front of him stood Bradley. Looking around, he realized he'd fallen asleep in his office again.

"I've been calling your name forever."

"Sorry, Brad."

"Davenport and I are ready to return to Conwy. Both of our men have been prepped, and Cordelia arrived last night from Conwy."

"How is she doing?"

"She's concerned. But she is more or less okay." Then, in waltzed Davenport. He wore a new suit, still black with a white tie, but it was neatly ironed and wrinkle free.

"Oh, Davy, I have something for you." Alistair rose and walked to his accent table opposite the door. He opened the drawer and pulled out a copy of *Venus and Adonis*, Shakespeare's first publication. He'd seen his brother's love for Shakespeare firsthand, and he absolutely loved that passionate Davenport.

"Here." Alistair placed the poem gently in Davenport's tired hands. Davenport's eyes lit up with joy, and he looked up at Alistair and did a little jump, like a child in a candy store.

"Thank you!" The excitement in Davenport's voice weaved its way to Alistair's heart. Alistair looked fondly at Davenport and patted him on the back.

"Godspeed, brother." He hugged Davenport close. He worried that Davenport would die fighting for Conwy. Davenport embraced his brother before slowly backing up and leaving the warehouse. Alistair was proud of Davenport. And if the plan worked, everything would turn out all right, but that was assuming there wouldn't be any hiccups in an extremely rushed plan.

The plan was simple: Assume defensive positions. The Jameson brothers had no idea when or where the Snappy Kings would attack; all they did know was that they would, so they had to be prepared at all times, day and night. Davenport was to head back before Bradley so as to not arouse suspicion. And the plan was airtight between the three brothers. No one else knew.

"You think he'll be all right?" Bradley asked.

"I think so."

Bradley nodded and looked out the window. An uneasy silence fell between the brothers; no one wanted to relive another war. Their bonds of brotherhood shrunk in that war. They couldn't afford for the bonds to shrink again. And Alistair, being the oldest, refused to be the last man standing.

"I think about Colburn all the time, Ally." Bradley slowly walked toward the big window behind Alistair. Alistair interlocked his fingers and focused on his knuckles, knuckles that were tired of being his.

"Me too."

"No you don't." Alistair couldn't be mad because he knew Bradley was right. Alistair didn't think about Colburn and actively resisted the memories brought forth about him. Of course, Alistair wanted Colburn back. He wanted Colburn alive.

"I dreamed about him last night."

"Yeah?"

"Remember his blue blanket? He carried that thing everywhere." Alistair laughed sadly. "I want little blue-blanket Colburn back."

"We all do. Colburn was the purest, warmest, and kindest soul to ever wander this earth, and those damned Germans took him."

"Old soldiers never die," Alistair whispered, barely audible to himself. He closed his eyes and thought back to the first time he ever said those four words.

"Friends, family, and loved ones. We're gathered here in a time of great sorrow, but let us not forget the love God has bestowed upon our dearly departed Colburn. Let us feel that happiness that fills the service, for God's fallen soldier lives on in eternal peace in Heaven. Let the Lord make marks with the purest human soul. And may You take Colburn to his resting place among the heroic warriors of our past. In Jesus's name, we pray. Amen.

"I find it fitting to read a poem, 'How Long, O Lord?' 'How long, O Lord, how long, before the flood of crimson-welling carnage shall abate? From sodden plains in West and East the blood of kindly men steams up in mists of hate, polluting Thy clean air; and nations great in reputation of the arts that bind the world with hopes of heaven, sink to the state of brute barbarians, whose ferocious mind gloats o'er the bloody havoc of their kind, not knowing love or mercy. Lord, how long shall Satan in high places lead the blind to battle for the passions of the strong? Oh, touch Thy children's hearts, that they may know hate their most hateful, pride their deadliest foe.'

"The grave war has claimed the lives of the greatest of men, but none so great as our dear Colburn. I speak not only from personal experience, but also on behalf of his comrades and his family. May the world long remember the sacrifice young Colburn has made and may the Great Lord be blessed with his presence up above. In Jesus's name, we pray. Amen." Father Romano stepped down from the pulpit. Alistair rose, tears in his eyes, and took his place.

"I have but one thing to say." Alistair looked up to the heavens, tears flowing, and pointed to the sky above. "Old soldiers never die, brother, old soldiers never die."

"Old soldiers never die," Bradley echoed. But Davenport, who was crying uncontrollably, couldn't say a thing. He wept in the misery of his split-second decision to save Bradley four years earlier. It was Alistair who decided to wait for a formal funeral until after the war had come to an end, and after he thought Davenport was ready. But clearly Davenport wasn't ready, as he wept with the rawest form of depression. But he finally managed to say it.

"Old soldiers never die," Bradley repeated. Alistair let his mind wander back to the present.

"Hey, Brad, do you want to go for a ride?"

Bradley snapped his head away from the window and faced his brother. "Are you serious?"

"Yes." It had been years since Alistair went riding with any of his brothers, but the afternoon air was perfect. The August sun spread warmly as a gentle breeze carried it right to the heart. The two brothers rose and weakly smiled. These were smiles where sadness outweighed happiness. The two brothers walked down the pristine staircase and onto the ground level. Once again, Alistair's presence brought an unnatural silence. Only this time he didn't embrace it, and he and Bradley headed for the door.

"Daddy!" Alistair whipped around and saw his daughter running toward him. He bent down and extended his arms, bringing his nirvana close. He elevated into a state of freedom from his worries.

"Where's Mary?" Bradley asked. Alistair side-eyed his brother.

But he knew that Bradley wanted to get out of the warehouse and into the woods. Alistair could feel his brother's enduring necessity to run through the pristine forest. Alistair let go of Esme. Alistair repeated the question.

"I don't know." Esme shrugged. Alistair stood and his eyes searched the room. But next to him, Bradley was getting impatient, something very uncharacteristic for Bradley. He tugged at Alistair's sleeve, almost dragging Alistair out.

"I'm sure she's tending to some business in the basement. Run along and have fun, Esme." She nodded and skipped off. After she was out of sight, Alistair turned and followed Bradley out. He just looked at his brother and sighed disappointedly at Mary's disappearance, putting his head down, as together they marched down the streets together, but in silence. Alistair's stables were not far away, but he felt like this walk would take forever. He just felt tense, like someone was waiting around every corner to kill him. To some extent, having the massive Bradley by his side made him feel safe. But at the same time, Bradley's extreme height caught the wandering eyes of the unknown. And it's always been the strangers that have forever negatively changed Alistair's life. Strangers forced him to fight, and strangers took Colburn from him. He wasn't about to let another unwanted stranger change his life for better or for worse.

"Brad, what's wrong?" Alistair couldn't help but notice his brother had fallen unusually quiet.

"Nothing."

Alistair recoiled at the coldness in his brother's voice. Alistair stopped walking. Something serious was going on with Bradley.

"Bradley—"

"Alistair, I said nothing, now can we move to the stables?"

"What's the rush?" Bradley stuck his hands into his pockets and marched forward. Reluctantly, Alistair trotted forward and said, "I hope Davy is okay."

"Shut up about Davenport, the world doesn't revolve around him." The bitter tone struck Alistair. He tried desperately to understand what was troubling Bradley, but nothing was all he could come up with. Alistair decided not to say anything more; sometimes silence is the best medicine.

Finally, the two arrived at the stables in complete silence. Alistair put his hand on Bradley's shoulder, and Bradley snapped his head around. He looked at Alistair with a heartbreaking look of regret, and his skin melted with Alistair's touch. Alistair furrowed his brow and pressed his lips into a thin line. Something seemed so off about Bradley. He was looking at Alistair like he was dead. Alistair picked his hand off of Bradley's shoulder and looked away.

"Brad, what's wrong?"

"You wouldn't understand." Bradley bit down on his lip. Alistair sighed and walked over to his stallion. Mighty Atlas stood, commanding the attention of every passerby. The beautiful beast carried his head high and proud.

"I might—"

"Your life is perfect!"

Alistair was not ready for this level of emotion coming from Bradley, who walked over to his mare, Ada. She was a magnificent horse in her own right. She may not have been as tall or pristine as Atlas, but she stood her ground. Her white coat shone in both the dark and the light. She carried herself like a warrior, strong yet light on her hooves.

"Perfect? If this is perfect, then heaven is hell." Alistair chuckled. He grabbed Atlas's saddle pad and began tacking him up. The horse turned his nose in search of scratches from Alistair, who eagerly reached out and stroked his horse's soft nose. Next to him, he heard Bradley sigh.

"It's Loretta. She's gone."

"Gone?"

"Gone. Two days ago she was drunk and started to yell about divorce. I told her to calm down. Last night I returned home and she wasn't there. Nor were any of her things."

"Oh, Brad, I'm so sorry."

"I asked my friends to do some digging. She bought a ticket for the SS *Duchess of York*. She's bound for Canada. That's not the worst part. She took the money that I was saving for when we someday had a child. She stole my money!"

"I have some buddies over in Canada. We can get her for robbery."

"No, let her run. Let the meek mouse run from its predator; it's so small anyway." Alistair nodded and grabbed his horse's reins, sliding the bit into Atlas's mouth. He walked Atlas out, but in reality he didn't need to. He and Atlas had such a tight bond, the horse would've followed Alistair. Alistair stopped and waited for Bradley. He looked his horse in the eye and pet him gently on his muscular side.

"Good boy," he whispered. Then he heard Bradley come trotting up.

"Come on, brother," Bradley taunted and began to canter away. Alistair chuckled and mounted his stunning creature. The duo began to trot, and Alistair's heartbeat matched his horse's gait. His horse was a powerful Andalusian and Bradley's mare a gorgeous Lipizzan imported from Spain. Davenport had a horse too, although his gelding was old. Davenport didn't ride his twenty-three-year-old Cleveland Bay horse, Rouge, anymore. Instead, he'd sit out in the paddock, and the two would rejoice in each other's company. Davenport had owned Rouge for a long time, nearly twenty years, and they had developed a bond only a great rider and a great horse could form. All the Jameson brothers found peace on horseback. Alistair wanted to get Davenport a new horse he could ride, but Davenport always resisted. So long as Rouge was alive, Davenport only wanted Rouge. Alistair respected his brother's loyalty to all things with a heartbeat.

"Come on, boy." Alistair clicked his tongue and his horse sped up, catching up with Bradley.

"Everything feels too calm," Bradley said.

"Come on, enjoy the peace while it lasts. Soon we will be at war, and peace will be hard to find." Alistair's horse trotted in line with Bradley's.

"No, you should always prepare for the unknown. No time to

be calm; after all, it's not the earthquake that gets you, it's the aftershocks."

"No, if you're always tense, you'll miss the events that make you human."

"I've been human, Ally, been there and done that. Guess what? I didn't like it. Men dropped around us like flies, Colburn was gunned down, Davy was forever changed, and us? We're no better than we were before. You and I are like every other man that fought—dead."

"Yet here we sit, atop beautiful beasts, alive as ever."

"How can you sit there so positive, when you know death will soon come?" Alistair hesitated. He had no idea why he was being so positive. But there was something about being with his brother in the woods on horseback. It made him feel young again; it was his connection to his childhood, the only connection that remained. He wanted to cherish what he had left of being a young boy, naive to what being human means. Humanity has a way of distinguishing itself from the natural world in destructive ways, ways that make children adults. Then afterward, positivity pops through and makes one value both the brightness and the shadows. One cannot dwindle too far in either extremity.

"Come on, let's go back." Bradley didn't wait for Alistair to respond. He turned Ada around and galloped away. Alistair rolled his eyes and turned Atlas around slowly. The horse whined at the disappointment of a short ride, but Alistair knew Bradley would enjoy riding more with Davenport's company. Alistair leaned forward and stroked Atlas's mane. Bradley had long galloped out of view, but Alistair didn't care. The world melted away, and it was just him and Atlas, nothing to worry about and nothing to fear.

"Alistair!" Bradley's yell was alarming, and fear shot its way through Alistair's veins, trying to reach his heart. He snapped his hand away from Atlas's neck and desperately asked his horse to gallop. Alistair tensed as he prepared for the worst.

"Alistair!" Bradley was barreling toward him and Atlas on a half-tacked horse. The second he saw Alistair, Bradley turned his horse around and galloped back toward the stables. Even the normally calm Atlas could sense something was wrong, as he flared his nose and pulled his ears back. The second the stables came into view, Alistair jumped off Atlas, leaving the poor creature very confused, and rushed to Bradley, who looked pale as a ghost and held a white sheet of paper in his hand.

"What's wrong?"

Bradley shoved the paper into Alistair's hand and kicked the wooden stall. "Why can't anything go our way, eh?"

Puzzled, Alistair looked hurriedly down at the note in his hands. It wasn't written in formal language, nor was it the letter of an educated person.

> *The Jamesons,*
>
> *As for Davenport's location, he's not where he is supposed to be. As for me? I know, but you don't. Mr. Jameson, I can learn much by listening to your speech. I want money. Meet me in the office.*

Alistair's heart broke as the fear in his veins carved its initials in his heart. He looked up at Bradley, and together the brothers mounted their horses and tore down the unpaved road and onto the street, a place where Alistair seldom rode his horse. But he didn't care. All he could think about was Davenport. He wasn't about to lose another brother.

CHAPTER 7

Atlas's hooves thundered down the road. They bounced off the harsh pavement and lit the street with panic. Ada's loud breathing added mayhem to the panic. The men and women on the streets fell into a deep silence; they dared not utter a word. The Jameson brothers' fearful fury poured from their bodies and oozed out onto the street. The people on the street shared the panic. Women hugged their children close, and the men froze in fear. There was nothing worse for the people than to see the brothers barreling toward the heart of the city on horseback. Alistair himself was as worried as the people watching, and Bradley was as scared as the children cowering. Davenport's safety was in jeopardy, and it dragged the brothers back in time, back to a dismal time. It pushed and pulled Alistair through his rocky childhood and threw him to his unstable younger years. The brief, yet mentally long, race to the warehouse washed Alistair's mind with the trauma from his life and painted his breath with fright. It was another moment Alistair felt helpless, hopeless, and powerless. In one quick motion, someone had swiped all the things Alistair relied on out from underneath him. He was free falling toward an area unknown, and he wanted out. The warehouse loomed into view. Its facade of wealth melted into raw severity. Neither

Alistair nor Bradley even bothered to stop their horses, but instead jumped off. Alistair wasn't as smooth as he was moments before and lost his footing as he slid off his horse, nearly hitting his head on the pavement. But that didn't matter. Bradley was already bursting through the doorway and looking right and left, weapon drawn.

"Which office?"

"Mine!" Alistair caught his breath before picking himself up off the ground and sprinting into the warehouse, not slowing down to prevent collisions with the workers. Anyone in his way was knocked down. When he reached the stairs, Alistair grabbed his gun and cocked it. Bradley waited at the top, gun close to his chin, and signaled for Alistair to stand on the other side of the doorway. Alistair sped up the steps and reached for the doorknob, but it was locked.

"Dammit!" Alistair pounded on the door. Bradley joined in, and together the brothers beat the door so loud that even the American militias of the past could hear.

"Whoever is in there, I'm warning you, open the door right now!"

"Did you lock it when you left?" Bradley spoke with an uneasy tone.

"No! I never lock it. I trust all my staff."

"Who else has a key?"

"No one. I have the only key in my pocket." Alistair reached his hand to his breast pocket, but his heart stopped. His fingers fumbled around, exploring every stitch, but there was nothing there; there was no key to be found. Alistair felt the blood drain from his face.

"I always keep my key here."

"Ally, where is the key?"

"I don't have it." Alistair felt defeated. He should've had the one thing he needed to save his brother, yet he had no clue where it was. Then he heard something sliding underneath the door. He looked down and saw a note, handwritten in his special ink. Cursing, he picked up the letter and began to read slowly.

I demand 100,000 pounds or else two things will be done. Don't forget, Mr. Jameson, I have the location of your Davenport, but I also have your location.

"Read this, Brad." Alistair flicked the note toward Bradley. Bradley grabbed it and hastily tore through the content. Once he comprehended what he had swiftly read, he hissed.

"One hundred thousand? Ally, I spent one hundred thousand for my men. We don't have this money. Our racing glory was shot out from beneath us, and we're struggling for Conwy."

"We have to pay."

"Ally, one hundred thousand pounds? This fight with the Snappy Kings isn't going to be cheap."

"We have to pay."

"And give into ransom demands? Once the community gets wind of this, they'll attack and hold our people hostage and expect to get away with it."

"We have to pay!"

"Alistair! We can't afford this politically, socially, or materially."

Alistair clenched his jaw so hard, his tongue began to bleed. But he knew Bradley was right. There was no way they could pay. Not only would it spell disaster for the Brassy Gats, but it would make them seem weak, hold them to lower standards on the pecking order. Alistair reared back and attempted to kick the door in, but it wouldn't budge. He had hired a special designer to manufacture the door in such a way that it was virtually impossible for anyone to intrude, and it was backfiring. Instead of keeping the unwanted out, it was keeping the unwanted in—pure irony. Yet, Alistair wasn't laughing; Alistair was desperate. The muscles in his face scrunched tightly and yelled, painting his face with the unmistakable anger Alistair usually tried to suppress. But now he was wearing his emotions like a name tag. Bradley was very much the same. They prioritized the fury that sprouted and ignored other feelings like sadness. Should despair roll in and attempt to take over, they'd become easy prey to tragedy. They'd rather be the hunters than the prey. Alistair and Bradley were once the prey, and they hated it.

"Lieutenant! We're surrounded."

Alistair snapped his head around, swiveling to see the high-stakes situation at hand. "Hold your ground!" he shouted over the constant gunfire. There wasn't anything they could do, and they were running low on ammo and food. They had been trapped for three days, and hope for the reinforcements they were promised was dwindling with each clink from the Germans' artillery. And to make matters worse, Alistair was without Colburn's soul. He only had Bradley on his right and was vulnerable on his left. But his platoon didn't have the manpower anymore to replace Colburn's position.

"Ally, it's not too late to retreat through the south side," Bradley said.

"It is. Not all of us will make it out that way. We can only hold our positions and wait for reinforcements."

"What are the chances they will come?"

Alistair turned his head away from Bradley. Both of them, as well as the rest of the platoon, knew the answer to Bradley's question; they weren't coming. But Alistair still held on to the hope that Davenport would pester his officers to send help; after all, Davenport was the hero of the Somme. Right now, that title earned him great levels of respect. But even Alistair knew Davenport couldn't do anything besides request, as it's vital to respect the superiors.

"Sir, the west group is completely out of ammo." Private Brighton rushed up to Alistair, his nerves flaring up and causing him to be unstable, so unstable he collapsed.

"Father!" Alistair called out for Father Romano, who had sacrificed his own safety to remain with the platoon.

The Father came running and saw the collapsed soldier—the youngest on Alistair's platoon—struggling to his knees, shaking and breathing very fast, as though every gasp was his last. The Father held the boy's hand and stroked his back. "Breathe, soldier, breathe. Focus on me, on my voice. What do you hear?"

"Guns," the soldier choked out, barely able to utter a single word.

"Good, what else?"

"Machine guns."

"Anything else?"

Brighton turned his head and looked around. His breathing began to slow, and although he was still shaking, his knees were steady enough to support him. "Birds? I think I hear birds."

"Good, good. Now what do you see?"

Brighton craned his neck and sat up higher. "Germans, Germans, Germans." Again he began to tremble.

"Look closer."

"I see . . ." Brighton turned his head and faced Alistair in the eyes. "My leader—our leader." He smiled. Alistair smiled too. He knelt next to the young soldier and put his hand on his shoulder.

"I see a strong force." The soldier slowly stood with the Father and Alistair supporting each of his arms. "I see a force devoid of hope but not grit. I see a force that won't give up. I see a platoon, mighty in all its glory, capable of finding a way out of this. I see a victory. I see a glimpse of hope, hope in the form of Lieutenant Jameson. So what if we're nearly dry of resources? I see we have a force stronger than the German forces."

Alistair felt Brighton shake him off and take three steps forward. The entire platoon had stopped what they were doing, save for the men working the machine guns, and turned to face Brighton. Alistair blushed. This was a speech Alistair should be giving, but he also found it natural to listen and let his inferiors have the spotlight. He was proud, in a fatherly way, of Brighton. Here was the mere eighteen-year-old, acting just like Alistair preached, rallying the hopeless troops.

"Some may be from Wales, London, Birmingham, or from small cities up north. Some may be twenty, twenty-two, even thirty. Some may be tall, like Big Bradley, or short, like Tiny Thomas. But we are kin. My own family will never see my rawness like you all have seen. So I'll be damned if we let this dire situation wreck our bonds!"

The men cheered. The sudden jolly sound threw the Germans off, as Alistair heard, for the first time, a momentary halt in the constant enemy fire. Alistair looked around his men. Everyone was united in a newfound glee in the midst of an acute survival situation. Brighton took a step back and looked toward Alistair. He felt the eyes of all his men on him, and there was no way he'd let any of them die. He wanted every single man looking at him alive.

"Ally, what's our plan?" Bradley asked. Every man looked at him, one eye filled with joy and the other filled with desperation. He looked at the horizon. He knew there was only one way out; they needed to rush the weakest point. They needed, single file, to run straight for the German Big Berthas. Insanely powerful but hard to maneuver and clunky, they were the weakest point in the German force. Alistair grabbed his gun and signaled for everyone to do the same. Some took their hand guns and some took rifles. Father Romano, of course, refused to touch a gun. As a result, Alistair placed him in the middle of the line of men, so as to offer him some form of protection. In the front, Alistair was to lead the troops, and in the back was Bradley.

Alistair slapped his brother on the shoulder. "For Colburn, brother. Godspeed."

Bradley nodded and Alistair confidently walked to the front of his men, but in reality he was terrified. None of the men had helmets on, as they had all placed their helmets around various spots in their makeshift trench to trick the Germans. If Alistair's plan failed, they'd be slaughtered, but if it succeeded, they could create confusion and force the Germans to fire toward their own. Once Alistair and his men were close enough to the two Big Berthas, the surrounding Germans ran the risk of shooting their own trying to shoot Alistair and his platoon. Each man had to sprint for his life, straight toward the middle space between the two Big Berthas. From his reconnaissance, he knew there were only two to four men there, and he had many more than that. All they needed was one point out, and then the men could zig and zag out of range. Alistair took a deep breath and turned around.

"On my call." His men nodded.

"One . . ." The men all tensed. They were two seconds away from a near suicide mission. But everyone realized that staying put would not only be a humiliating defeat, but suicide too.

"Two . . ." The men grabbed their guns and got down into a runner's stance. Alistair had tried his best to organize the men by speed, the faster ones in the back and the slower ones toward the front.

"Three . . ." This was it. There were only mere nanoseconds between life and death. Alistair flared his nostrils and squeezed his thighs.

"Go!" Alistair jumped out of the trench and sprinted faster than he ever had before. It took the Germans a couple of seconds to register what was happening and another few seconds to react. That was all Alistair and his men needed to suddenly have a very miniscule advantage, but an advantage nonetheless. Alistair put his finger on the trigger and fired forward. Behind him, his men staggered just enough to fire their own guns right to the area Alistair was firing. All around him, German shouts poisoned his ears and bullets whizzed past. Every single bullet that flew by his ears made Alistair fight harder than he ever had to ignore his instinct and keep running. In front of him, the three Germans between the useless Big Berthas grabbed their rifles hung over their backs and they fired, but it was too late. Alistair and his men came out of the trench gunning, and their bullets reached their targets. But Alistair sensed doom; he felt a bullet, a flash of gold, whizzing through the sky, carrying with it the weight of a thousand horses. It took his brain nanoseconds to register he was going down. His body, however, didn't have enough time to react. Alistair heard the crunch of bone and flesh give way to the force of lead. Alistair collapsed in pain. He shouted and grimaced, and his whole body came crashing to the earth. But he had done his job for his men and, in horrible pain, ordered his men to push on. He tried to claw his way forward, but the pain ricocheted from every cell, and blood poured from his wound. He clenched his teeth and felt his gums groan with the weight of his bite. There were no words to describe how he felt. His vision flashed from white to black, clear to blurry, yet his hearing remained untouched. He heard his men run toward their freedom. Alistair looked up and realized he'd die should he succumb to the pain. Forcing his arms to function, he pushed himself up. But with each ounce of force he expelled, his pain increased tenfold. He shouted and cried in agony, but yet still he rose. Then suddenly, he felt the strong grasp of someone on his arm. He shouted again, as the pain only increased. His breathing became unsteady, to the point where he couldn't even cry. He felt his head fall back, and he lost all control of his muscles. He could feel his heels create an unappreciated drag in the dirt as Bradley desperately pulled Alistair through the oncoming fire and the chaos. Alistair, however, could only barely make out the unmistakable sky. His vision blurred and his breathing was shallow. The sharp pain burned; his wound felt hot. The sensations that traveled up and down his abdomen were indestructible, and he felt like someone had poured lava into his chest.

"Go, go, go!" Alistair could hear Bradley shouting. Someone was turning around and running back toward Alistair and Bradley.

"Father! Turn around!" Alistair could hear the desperation in Bradley's voice, yet he knew that Father Romano would never leave him and Bradley. Suddenly, he felt his feet leave the ground and Bradley sped up. Alistair attempted to let out a cry, as the movement burned his chest. He thought he could feel the screams of pain escape his mouth, but he wasn't sure. He *was* sure that the sound of German machine guns was quieter, and then finally, Bradley came to a steady trot instead of a sprint for his life.

"Father, how's it looking?" Alistair could barely hear his brother's voice, but the worry in it was easily heard.

"The bullet is lodged in his chest, right below his rib."

"And?"

Father Romano sighed. "And if he doesn't receive immediate medical attention, he'll die." Alistair didn't have enough energy to feel the fear usually associated with death. But he knew Bradley had the energy, and he felt the ground shake as Bradley sank to his knees. Yet, even though Bradley was on his knees, he felt the ground continue to shake and rumble. Alistair felt like he was dying;

sprawled out on the ground, barely conscious, he was ready to let himself go. He felt the whimsical presence of Colburn, yet the shaking in the ground only intensified. He heard muted voices and pleas for help. The rumble and the shaking got closer still, and Alistair didn't know why. He looked up at his brother, who was frantically signaling to someone. He heard the footsteps of men coming closer. Suddenly, his glossy vision caught the glimpse of men leaning over him. They wrapped his wound with gauze and he cried out, as it stung. Alistair tried to reach out to Bradley, but he barely had the energy to move a finger. Yet, at that moment, he remembered his men. He didn't remember anyone going down like he did, and he hoped they were all alive.

"Brad, Br—" Alistair panted. He couldn't even get his brother's name out.

"Shhh, you'll be okay, Ally." Bradley reached out and stroked Alistair's hair.

Alistair felt oddly comforted. "Brad." Again, that's all Alistair could say.

"Shhh, everyone's okay. You were the only victim. Ally, you did it! You saved us."

Alistair felt what he thought was a smile creep up on his pale face.

"Now what do we do, Ally?"

Alistair shook his head and snapped back to the present. There was limited time, as Bradley's men would soon arrive in Conwy without a leader. They'd cause chaos, like drunken men without one sober man. Then he heard that noise again, the sound of disaster scraping the floor. This time Bradley reached down and snatched the note off the floor. Again the villain was scared to share its voice with the brothers.

"It says, "*I'm waiting, boys.*" Bradley looked up to Alistair, fear melting the anger off his face. Alistair reached out and placed his hand on Bradley's shoulder. The duty of a lieutenant was to put his valuable soldiers before himself. After the fear was comforted away, Bradley snapped back into his place of anger. "Coward! Face us man to man!"

"Coward!" Alistair spat. Pounding his fist on the door was all in vain; the door refused to give in to the demands from its creator. Alistair was livid, yet still there was no sound from inside, only the sound of pen on paper. Alistair was not accustomed to this kind of warfare, warfare in which one side toyed with the other. To Alistair, he took this to be an indirect surrender. And again, the only response they got was in the form of a letter. Alistair stomped on it and dragged his foot back to his body, thereby taking the disgraceful note with it. He bent down and began to read.

> *"Old soldiers never die?" We'll see about that. Mr. Jameson and Mr. Jameson, I've a new saying: Old soldiers die. Your brother is an old soldier, and he will die. Give me the money or else your entire group will be over. Old soldiers die.*

That was it. Something within him snapped, and he was ready to beat up that bastard. He chuckled as he slowly turned and walked as far as he could before he reached the stair's banister. Rocking back and forth, he suddenly exploded. Running full speed toward the door, he leaped into it. The door splintered and came crashing down. Alistair, stumbling and falling with the force of the impact, was oblivious to the sharp pain in his shoulder. Bradley came shouting into the office, gun drawn and ready to protect Alistair, but soon put his weapon down upon entering. Alistair looked up, dusting himself off. What he saw, specifically *who* he saw, surprised him. That's the worst part about betrayal—it always comes from someone one cares about. Both Alistair and Bradley were completely coldcocked. Their villain was a quintessence of Judas.

CHAPTER 8

Alistair breathed deeply and clenched his fists. He could hear the maniacal chuckles coming from his desk along with Bradley's angry snarls. Alistair shoved the planks from the fallen door off his shoulder and rose, shell-shocked. He took two steps and turned to face Bradley, whose piercing eyes never left the aggressor. Bradley stood, still as a statue, not moving a muscle. It seemed as though even his heart failed to beat. Then all of a sudden, Bradley came to life. He exploded forward, barreling straight toward Mary. Alistair jumped forward and grabbed his brother, restraining him.

"Brad! Calm down! Breathe, brother!" Alistair struggled to hold his brother back.

"She has Davenport!" Alistair pushed his brother toward the back of the room.

"I know, Brad. Believe me, I'd have shot her by now, but she has leverage. She's more valuable alive than dead."

"Then I'll shoot her after," Bradley hissed. There were certain things Alistair knew forced his brother into an uncontrollable wave of fury, and anyone harming his family was one of them.

"You and me both." Alistair could practically hear Bradley's teeth grind with the intensity of his anger, and Alistair knew his brother was trying to restrain his rare impulses for the sake of their precious brother. They looked each other in the eye and matched their breathing cycles, feeling their roots of humanity calm them. Taking a deep breath, Alistair turned around and once again assumed his intimidating walk.

"Mary, I don't know what to say."

"Then allow me to speak. I know where Davenport is, and I know that you're alive. I'll have no shame in turning in the remaining all-mighty Jameson brothers. Mr. Jameson, how stupid are you to trust your daughter with someone evil enough to kidnap your brother?"

Alistair looked Mary dead in the eyes and tried to breathe. He couldn't let Mary get under his skin, as hard as it was. "Congratulations, you tricked the both of us. Is that what you want?"

"Not at all, Mr. Jameson. I want money."

"Money is the plague that infects us all, why would you want some of that?" Alistair took two steps toward Mary. She sat on his desk, crossing her legs, and played with her hair. She wasn't concerned at all. She knew the power she had over two of the most powerful men in all of England.

"Mr. Jameson, I don't need your pity."

"We don't need your life," Bradley spat.

"Oh?"

Alistair eyed his brother. "Brad, a word?" Alistair grabbed his brother's arm and they turned and slowly walked toward the back of the room.

"A house divided against itself won't stand," Mary said, taunting the brothers.

Bradley turned around and rushed right at Mary, stopping face-to-face with her. "Before you play with fire, do think twice," Bradley threatened.

Alistair yanked his brother's shoulders, and they retreated back to the corner. "Calm down, Brad," Alistair said in a hushed whisper. He wasn't about to let Mary hear their conversation.

"Why should I?"

"Because you and I both know she's enjoying this."

"I'm intimidating her."

"No, no you're not. You're playing her game." Alistair chuckled. "If anything, you're acting like Davenport. Brad, I need you to act like that composed Bradley I know."

Bradley put his hands on his hips and sighed, swaying under Alistair's cold stare. "Don't lecture me, Ally. I've seen your uncontrollable temper, yet no one checks you. You, of all people, should know anger can be beneficial."

"Not now, Bradley. Sometimes war is a time of sheer chaos. This isn't; this is a time that calls for calm strategy." Alistair wanted to continue his conversation with Bradley, but he needed to get back to Mary or her confidence would only soar.

"I trusted you, Mary."

"Oh?"

"I left you alone with Esme."

"She's wonderful. Such a pity her daddy isn't more like her."

"I value individuality."

"Individuality is just a suggestion, Mr. Jameson."

"You think so? Well, maybe I should fire all of my female workers and replace them with men. I'll start right here: You're fired."

"Mr. Jameson," Mary said, laughing. "I wouldn't do that."

"I'm in the authority to fire you."

"Poor Mr. Jameson. You don't really know how powerless you are. I have the power. It'll just be you and your brother, Mr. Jameson. Don't you think two is a lot lonelier than one?"

"I'm not sure I understand, Mary."

"I'll leave you brokenhearted by the end of the day."

"My heart is already broken."

Bradley took another step forward, standing right next to his brother. "We're Jamesons, Mary. There's nothing you can do to paralyze us."

"Is that so, Mr. Jameson?"

"My brother speaks the truth, Mary. You can take a Jameson away from us but you can't take the Jameson out of us." Alistair felt Bradley reach out and pat him on the shoulder. He looked at

Bradley, who returned his gaze. Together, they formed a dynamic duo. For two years it had been Alistair and Bradley who risked their lives together, mourned together, fought together, and prevailed together. They knew hardships, they knew heartbreak, and they knew defeat, but they always had each other. Alistair and Bradley saw each other almost die numerous times, yet they always saw themselves survive. It had taken them years to be able to think about the death of their younger brother Colburn but they had each other to fall on. They had Davenport, too, but Davenport still couldn't think about his older brother. Every hardship the brothers faced, they could always count on each other to make things better. Alistair reached out and held on to Bradley's forearm, signifying their resilience.

"Mary—" Alistair was interrupted by a ringing. He looked toward the end of his desk where his phone rang, further intensifying the atmosphere. Alistair, Bradley, and Mary all stared at the phone. No one moved an inch. Then, at the same time, everyone jumped toward the phone. Mary, being the closest, got their first, but Bradley's big body knocked her away from it, and she lost her grasp.

"Grab it, Ally!" Bradley cornered Mary away from the phone. She still pushed and fought like a wild animal, desperately trying to reach the phone before the two brothers could. She uselessly threw her body over Bradley's arms and tried to drag her way to the phone, but Alistair already was picking up the handset. He chuckled as he lifted the phone to his ear.

"Hello?" Alistair heard someone on the end of the line and gasped. He nearly dropped the phone. "Yes, right away. He'll be coming, we both will. Yes, the two of us." Alistair hung up the phone and cleared his throat. He smoothed out his suit and straightened his tie.

"Mary, Mary, Mary. I don't like my time to be wasted, and you have done just that. Brad, we must go."

"But what about Davy?" Bradley pointed to Mary, who by now had slunk to the back of the room and was trembling against a bookshelf.

"Oh, he just called. He was wondering when you were coming, Brad, because he'd gotten word of a large camp just outside of Conwy. The Snappy Kings appear to be preparing an attack."

"What?"

"Yes."

"What? So this"—Bradley whipped around and stood, shaking with rage—"this animal is lying? And that war is going to break out tomorrow morning?"

"Apparently." Bradley chuckled and turned his head. Alistair looked at his brother and nodded. In sync, the two brothers drew their guns and fired. Both bullets whizzed to their point-blank target. Each bullet struck home, one right between Mary's eyes, the other right through her heart. She cowardly slumped against the books, dead. Only once she was dead did the two brothers begin to panic.

"Ally, are we going to make it in time?" Bradley started to pace.

Alistair scratched his head and trotted to the door. "Come on. Let's go." Alistair hovered in the doorway, waiting for his brother to calm down and come with him.

"We'll never make it by horseback."

"We're not traveling on horseback, Brad."

"Well, we can't take our cars, they're too recognizable."

"We're taking the train."

"The train?" Bradley checked his watch. "They're not running at this time."

"They'll run for us." Alistair turned and sped away, not waiting for Bradley. He heard Bradley jog to catch up. The two brothers, somewhat relieved of their anxiety, hastily left the warehouse. Alistair looked up and down the road and was relieved to see their horses standing across the street. They had been in such a hurry, they had left the horses untethered. Once Atlas and Ada noticed their owners, they came trotting up, confused. Alistair reached out and grabbed his horse's reins, nuzzling his head. He then mounted his beautiful stallion and waited for Bradley, who was having a harder time, as Ada was acting skittish. She was afraid of the street, afraid of the inhumanity that crawled through every crack in the pavement. Alistair couldn't blame her, as it had taken a war for him to get used to barbaric views.

"Easy, girl." Bradley mounted his shining mare, but she wasn't pleased. She backed up and reared, trying to get Bradley off. Alistair strode over and reached out, trying to grab the side of her reins to help Bradley control her. He finally snatched them and held on tight. Ada tried, but she had a hard time rearing. Alistair clicked his tongue and brought Atlas to a walk, calming down Ada. Alistair dropped her reins and the two brothers continued calmly to the train station.

"Ally?"

Alistair turned. His brother stopped in the middle of the road. "Yes?"

"You can't go, Ally. You need to stay here. You have a daughter to look after, and if you're spotted in Conwy our plan will burn before our eyes."

"Cordelia is looking after Esme." Alistair clicked his tongue and Atlas sped up to a canter. He reached out and stroked his horse's muscular neck. "Come on, Brad. We'll discuss this more on the train. But right now we need to hurry, or we'll miss the start of the drama."

"This isn't a play, Alistair."

"The world is a show, Brad. We're all just characters."

"People are going to die."

"Yes."

"One of us could die."

Alistair put his head down and asked Atlas to gallop, which he did with no resistance. Together they flew down the road and passed numerous people, all looking on with a mix of confusion and fear. Soon, Ada and Bradley ran along Alistair and Atlas, and the pairs ran in unison. Their power of unity stopped the leaves mid-fall, the wind mid-gust, and the barbarism mid-destruction. They needed to get to Conwy, and as a unified force there was nothing they couldn't conquer. Although, one unified force versus another can create a massive force of utter destruction.

Humanity and humanity collide to push the world to inhumanity. Finally, the station loomed into view. It wasn't the same as a traditional station, as it had been recently built just for the convenience of the Brassy Gats, but it was a station nevertheless. Alistair and Bradley slowed their horses and dismounted them properly, giving them to the station's stable boy.

"Cheers." Alistair and Bradley nodded their heads and jogged toward the engineer, who sat in the locomotive. Alistair jumped up and grabbed on to the railing and knocked on the window.

"Engineer! Urgent business, we need to go to Conwy right now."

"Mr. Jameson, we're not running right now."

"We need to go to Conwy *right now.*" Alistair stressed the urgency of his words. Bradley, who had remained on the ground, tapped Alistair on the back. Alistair turned.

"Ally, I think you dropped this." Bradley reached out and handed Alistair his gun, making sure the engineer could see the weapon.

"Thanks, Brad." Alistair turned toward the engineer. "Shall we get going?"

"Of course, right away, Mr. Jameson." The engineer reached forward and began shoveling coal into the engine's fire box. The train shook as it roared to life.

"Better hop on now, Mr. Jameson. We're headed nonstop to Conwy. We should be there in a matter of hours."

"Thank you, engineer." Alistair hopped off the side of the locomotive and signaled to Bradley. The two brothers climbed aboard.

There was no one else on the train, only the three of them. Alistair walked up and down the rows of seats before settling into a seat by the window. He watched as the clouds began to open up and a silent drizzle painted the sky. Bradley cleared his throat, and Alistair turned his head away from the view and toward his brother.

"Ally, I don't think you should stay in Conwy."

"It's my battle to fight."

"It's our battle, Ally."

"Our battle that I need to fight too."

"Look, I respect your bravery, but think about your brothers' lives. Should your existence come to the attention of Dirkson, Eastaughffe, or Cromwell, we're screwed. Our plan walks a delicate line, and we're just hovering on the edge of failure."

"Davy is our youngest brother, Brad. This was an eye-opener. I'm not going to sit around with his wife and my daughter while you two put your lives on the line."

"This isn't smart."

"Maybe, maybe not."

"Alistair, too much is at stake to gamble like this."

"Too much is at stake to not gamble." Alistair had already made up his mind. Their plan had fallen apart before they ever advanced past the first step. Alistair turned his head and looked out the window again. The drizzle from only minutes ago faded into a misty haze, covering everything.

"How's the shoulder?" Alistair looked down at his torn suit. He had been too distracted to notice he was bleeding from ramming down the door. He moved his arm up and down, and thankfully, there was little pain.

"Fine." Alistair turned his attention to nature once again. He should've said goodbye to Esme, but in the heat of the moment, he hadn't had the chance. He was sure Cordelia would understand, but still it didn't sit right with him. After all, the brothers could be traveling to their deaths.

"Please reconsider, Ally."

"I've made up my mind," Alistair snapped.

"Calm down, Ally. You said it yourself—calm strategy."

"This is war, Brad. I don't fancy losing." Alistair turned so his body faced Bradley's. The two brothers looked tired and disheveled, yet they were stronger than ever. Each fueled with rage and hope, both of their livelihoods rested on the battle for Conwy.

"No one does."

"Are you going to call Dirkson?"

"I think it's best if I ride out to the camp of the Snappy Kings' men and strike a deal with Dirkson face-to-face, seeing as I never had the chance to call him."

"You think that'll work?"

"Do we have a choice?"

"No, Brad, we don't." Alistair sighed. He never liked battle plans formulated around the question, "Do we have a choice?" because he knew the low success rate. He much preferred well-thought-out plans with at least sufficient backup plans. Alistair knew what he and Bradley agreed on in the desperate ride to Conwy would be what's final. And they couldn't risk calling Davenport from a public and unstable telephone such as the one on the train.

"Brad, I'll fill Davy in on the revised plan, and you head straight to the camp. Borrow one of Old Jim's horses. He can't ride them anymore, and he practically begs people to ride them so the horses stay fit."

"Okay. What's going to happen while I'm at Dirkson's camp?"

"Well, if you can buy us some time, we can set up ambushes and traps all throughout Conwy. We can get the men ready in defensive positions in the front and the back exits of the town. I'll take command of your army, and Davy can still command his."

"And if I can't buy you time?"

"Then all hell will break loose."

"I'll try my best. Oh, and Ally, how should I report back to you what's happening with Dirkson and his men?"

Alistair furrowed his brow and hesitated. He knew Bradley couldn't risk calling, so the only other option would be by mail.

"Hide it somewhere in the horse's tack. Surely, Dirkson will let you bring the horse back to its owner every day. From there, I'll take the letter from the tack and bring it back to a place where Davy and I can read it."

"Ally, this plan has a lot of holes in it. So many things could go wrong, all of which result in my death."

Alistair took a deep breath. He ran the same scenarios through his head, and he, too, knew that should anything go wrong, the first to fall would be Bradley. It was their responsibility to keep Bradley alive.

"Breathe, brother. You're going to be a hero to Brassy Gats and everyone on our payroll; all you need to worry about is your side of the plan, and I'll worry about mine."

"That's a lie; you'll worry about my life."

Alistair put his hand on his brother's shoulder and nodded. Of course Alistair was going to worry about Bradley, but he knew he needed his mind sharp. War is a game of wits and manpower. All Alistair had was the wits.

CHAPTER 9

"Attaboy, Alistair." Alistair giddily bounced up and down on his tiny pony, Georgie. He went around in circles as his pony went no faster than a trot. To Alistair, he felt like he was flying. The wind blew, albeit slowly, his bangs to either side of his face. He heard birds chirping in the distance and welcomed the warm sunlight. It has been raining all day, and the sky finally turned calm. Alistair laughed with each breath he took. He absolutely loved it.

"Like this, Daddy?" Alistair clicked his tongue, and his pony sped up only slightly. Alistair was too small to fully control his family's obedient old pony, but that didn't matter. Georgie didn't mind having Alistair atop his back. And Alistair certainly loved being on top of Georgie.

"I want a turn, Daddy!" Bradley came bounding out of the house, running into their father's arms.

"No! My riding lesson," cried Alistair.

Their father chuckled and put Bradley down. He pointed to the stables and bent down so he was on Bradley's level. "You have your own pony, Bradley."

"But she's a she! I want a boy horse."

"What's wrong with Rainy? You love her." Their father collected Bradley's hand, and together they walked over to the stable where their father had already tacked up Rainy. She was an old pony, too, and much like Georgie, she couldn't care less who was riding her. She was a diligent mare, and she and Bradley got along very well. Bradley stomped his foot and pointed to Alistair. Alistair brought Georgie to a stop, or tried to, but he was having a hard time pulling back on the reins hard enough. Georgie whinnied before coming to a stop and bending down to eat the grass. Alistair lit up as Bradley finally emerged from the stable, riding Rainy, although because Bradley was so young, their father held on to the bridle.

"Mack!" Alistair looked toward their house. The windows glistened in the sunlight, and the flowers stood tall and proud in front of the back porch. Alistair's mother stood in the doorway. She was pregnant with Colburn, and every day she prayed for her son's healthy delivery. At that time, many women and children died in childbirth.

"Mack!" she cried again. Their father let go of Rainy's bridle as he jogged over to his wife. Alistair could hear their voices, but they were too far away for him to make out what they were saying. Alistair turned toward Bradley and laughed. His brother sat, for the first time, on horseback without his father guiding the creature.

"Come on, Brad!"

"I'm scared, Ally."

"Come on, Brad, it's not that hard."

Bradley hesitated, but he clicked his tongue, and Rainy slowly took a few steps forward. Alistair clicked his tongue, and Georgie more confidently sped up, albeit nothing more than a lazy prance.

"I'm doing it!" Bradley shrieked. His movements, while physically small, were huge. Alistair reached forward and stroked Georgie's mane, as the four of them walked around in a slow, but independent, circle.

"Ally, I've decided that mares are the best. I only want mares." Bradley beamed.

"Stallions are better!" Alistair mocked. He laughed at his brother's quick change of mind.

"Mares!"

"Stallions!"

Before Bradley could get another retort in, they heard the chugging of engines off in the distance. "What's that, Ally?"

Alistair shrugged and said, "Daddy said they're carts without the horses." Alistair strained his eyes, trying to see the new invention. He was fascinated by the clanking sound of wheels without the expected snorting sound of nickering horses. He let his gaze settle on the paddock, where his parents' massive Clydesdales were playfully roaming around. One day he hoped to ride them, but he was too small. They, too, were very docile and seemed to like Alistair and Bradley.

"Huh?"

"He called them cars."

"Cars." Bradley stared off into the distance. "Cool!"

Alistair followed his brother's gaze in an attempt to see the car. He heard tires roll effortlessly over the dirt road. He wanted to see this car, as he hardly believed it. He didn't want the cars to take away the Clydesdales, but he wasn't certain the car was real and not a fantasy.

Clank, clank, clank.

Clank. Alistair jerked his head up. Looking around, it took him a second to recognize he was en route in his desperate dash to Conwy.

"Why didn't you wake me, Brad?"

"You looked so peaceful. Peace is hard to come by these days."

Alistair rubbed his eyes and shook his head. He needed to wake his mind up and shove the drowsiness out.

"Were you dreaming?"

"Yes."

"Fascinating. What does it even mean to dream? Perhaps that's our subconscious creating a life it would rather see us in. What did you dream about?" Bradley turned his head to face

Alistair, and for the first time, Bradley thought his brother looked tired.

"The first time you rode Rainy without dad guiding her."

Bradley chuckled. "She was quite the pony, wasn't she?"

"You used to hate riding her."

"Mares are the best." Bradley chuckled and slapped his brother on the shoulder.

"Those were good days, weren't they?"

"Yes, yes they were. Those were the days before Mom moped around all day and Dad drank his emotions away."

Alistair looked down at his hands. After their mother gave birth to Davenport, she fell into a deep depression. She wouldn't leave her room for days at a time, and their father was enraged by this. He began drinking every day, and his temper spiked. They were never the same again.

"Brad, you ready?"

"No, but no one is ever ready."

"Don't worry."

"Easy for you to say."

Alistair turned his head and noticed the scenery had changed. The birds had been replaced with seabirds, and the air smelled of fish. They were close.

"How long was I asleep?"

"About two hours."

Alistair cursed. Those two hours would've been more valuable if he had been awake. He and Bradley should've polished their rushed plan, but now the most they could do was slap on a halfhearted coat of paint and make it look pretty, knowing full well that the paint would chip quickly.

"Ally"—Bradley looked Alistair dead in the eyes—"we need to discuss something."

"Good idea. Let's review the plan and finalize it."

"No, Ally. What happens if you die? Which brother gets to take control, Davy or me?"

"That's not—"

"You don't know."

Alistair sighed. He knew that Bradley was right; there was a chance Alistair would die.

"Well . . ." Alistair thought long and hard. "Davy should take control during the fighting. We can't risk you leaving your position within the enemy's heart." Bradley nodded, and Alistair let out a sigh of relief, as his brother understood how little room for error there was in this rushed conflict.

"And after?"

Alistair didn't know how to answer that question. He couldn't leave total control in Davenport's impulsive hands, yet he couldn't leave total control in the hands of Bradley, who was too rational. He was the perfect mix between his two brothers, a clear figure for leading the Brassy Gats.

"Ally?"

"Both of you. Davy is too impulsive to lead alone, and you're not impulsive enough."

"And that's a bad thing?"

"No risk, no reward," Alistair said flatly. He knew that this war was a risk Bradley would've been hesitant to engage in, but something Davenport would've instigated prematurely. He hoped that, should he die, his brothers could remember that this organization is a family business and can be run with two co-leaders. The last thing he wanted was a civil war. A civil war would not only ruin the Brassy Gats, but it would also divide Burford. Part of his responsibility was to protect the citizens of Burford from any threats, granted they respect the Brassy Gats.

"Fair enough."

Alistair reached out and grabbed his brother's shoulders. Bradley was so understanding, so mature. Had Davenport been on the receiving end of Alistair's words, he would've freaked out. "Let's not think about this, Brad." Alistair turned his head and shuddered. He tried his hardest to be strong and fearless, but alas, he was only human. Nothing scared him more than death, be it his own or his family's. He had had his brush with death, and he hated it.

"Ally." Bradley reached out and shook his brother's shoulder.

"Everything's going to be all right."

"Yes." Alistair cleared his throat. "I wonder how Davy is doing."

Bradley nodded and proposed that Davenport was, at the worst, confused. Alistair agreed, but he feared something more sinister; he feared Davenport was scared. Fright is a good thing, but in someone as impulsive as Davenport, fright can be deadly; a wild animal backed into a corner is the most dangerous, and Alistair knew Davenport played the role of a wild animal well. He couldn't imagine what had happened under the trenches. He couldn't even bear to think about it, because if the trenches were hell, what did that make the tunnels? Alistair didn't want to know the answer. The odds of death in the Great War were high, but even higher underground. The threats Davenport and his comrades had to face ranged from bad to worse. Davenport had faced all things evil, and the one day he emerged was the day the devil decided to laugh.

Alistair jerked forward as the train came to an abrupt stop about ten miles away from the station. They'd made it to Conwy. Alistair sighed as he put his hands on his thighs and slowly rose. He felt his heart pound, but he could sense Bradley's heart was pounding harder. The strong bonds of brotherhood didn't need words to communicate their messages.

"I should go if I'm to make it to the camp before midnight." Bradley offered a half-reassuring smile.

"I know, and Brad?"

"Yes?"

"Don't forget who you're fighting for."

Bradley reached out and squeezed Alistair's shoulder. "I'll never forget."

Alistair nodded. "Godspeed, brother. Remember, old soldiers never die." Alistair stretched out his hand and Bradley took it. He pulled Bradley close and slapped him on the back. Both brothers feared the same thing: that they might never see each other again.

"Godspeed, Ally. Give my love to Davy."

"I will."

"Old soldiers never die."

Bradley turned and walked to the front of the car before looking back over his shoulder and weakly waving. Alistair nodded back, and Bradley disappeared as he stepped off the train. Alistair was now alone. He made his way to the door and watched his brother walk alone alongside the train tracks, the sunset framing Bradley's tall build. Alistair only hoped his brother would be able to gain the trust of his enemy. *Keep your friends close but your enemies closer,* Alistair reminded himself.

"Mr. Jameson, I best be going."

Alistair turned around. He was so lost in his own head, he hadn't heard the engineer approach him.

"Thank you, engineer." Alistair reached into his pocket and took out all the coins he had and placed them in the engineer's hands.

"That's very generous, Mr. Jameson."

"It's the least I can do." Alistair slapped him on the shoulder and stepped off the train. He walked away from the rails and sat down on a nearby rock. The foliage and the trees sheltered Alistair from the prying eyes of the public, but they couldn't shelter his mind from paranoia. Every part of the plan was delicately placed and extremely fragile. Alistair shook his head and reached his arms over his head, calming himself down. He stood and put his hands in his pockets and pulled his hat over his forehead. He put his chin up and confidently trotted down the tracks. If he didn't believe in himself and his brothers, the plan would inevitably collapse. He looked at the tracks as he walked past, fixating on their silhouette, as the sun had set and he could barely see in front of his own feet. The dark didn't scare him, but he didn't like it. He only knew one man who loved the darkness, because he seemed to be able to see without light. He would take his horse, Ranger, who was an old horse now living next to Rouge, and fly through the woods in the night.

"Slow down, Colburn! I can't see," Alistair called. He was riding Georgie as he followed Colburn atop Ranger.

"Slow poke!"

"Georgie can't see! I can't see!"

Colburn chuckled. He knew he could see better than his older brothers, and Colburn loved it. He would run around at night scaring his brothers and parents alike.

"Come on, Ally!"

Alistair was frustrated, but his brother's calming voice nullified his anger. He couldn't stay mad at Colburn forever, as his emerald-green eyes pleaded for forgiveness and his curly ginger hair always bounced with Colburn's energy.

"Ally!" Colburn chanted as he urged Ranger deeper into the woods.

"We're going to get lost."

"No, I can see!"

"But can you remember?" Alistair could only follow the sound of Ranger's young, lively hooves bouncing off the dirt or occasionally snapping a twig. He and Colburn weren't supposed to be out this late, but their parents were sound asleep, so no one would notice. Bradley, who feared what he couldn't see, had agreed to stand guard and cover for his brothers should he need to. It was the beginning of their daredevil acts, acts that soon transitioned into their adult life. Colburn chuckled and urged his horse to run faster.

"No!" Colburn laughed.

Alistair could feel Georgie getting tired. He was an old gelding, and he couldn't keep up with the young Ranger.

"Ally, look!" Colburn brought Ranger to a sudden stop. Alistair yanked on his reins, and Georgie jerked back. Neither Alistair nor Georgie expected the leading duo to come to such an abrupt stop. Every day, Colburn surprised Alistair, as he was such a great rider for such a young child. Alistair had no doubt he'd watch his brother become a professional rider.

"Look!" Colburn jumped off Ranger and happily skipped next to Ally. "A river!"

Alistair strained his eyes, but he couldn't see any river. But the more he focused, the more he could hear the bubbling sounds of water. He hopped off Georgie and guided him down to the riverbank. The tired old pony eagerly lapped up the water. Alistair turned, suddenly realizing he was alone. He felt sweat drip down his forehead, and he desperately whirled around in search of his brother.

"Colburn!" All was silent. He reached out and grabbed Ranger's reins and was even more frightened that his brother's horse was unmounted.

"Boo!"

Alistair jumped backward, and Colburn collapsed to the ground in a fit of unstoppable laughter.

"Colburn! You frightened me." Alistair took three deep breaths and pushed Colburn in a brotherly display of affection. Colburn tried to push Alistair back, but he wasn't big enough. Alistair laughed and he wrestled Colburn to the ground. The two brothers rolled around ground in the dirt, and Alistair decided to let Colburn win. Colburn jumped up triumphantly and danced around in a circle.

"I win, I win!" Colburn stood in front of Alistair and flexed. Alistair pushed his brother, who lost his balance and stumbled backward. Alistair reached out, but Colburn's momentum pulled him down, too, and they landed, unexpectedly, in the river. Colburn laughed even harder and splashed his brother. Alistair gasped and splashed his brother back. The two broke into a synchronized laugh, and Alistair could feel his brother's massive smile. After their laughing fit, the two brothers reached the bank and tried to get out, but Alistair slipped on a rock and fell back into the river. Colburn couldn't contain his laughter.

"Ow!" Alistair shook his head and realized he was on the ground. Looking behind him, he saw a massive rock sticking out of the earth, waiting to trip the idiots who couldn't see it. Alistair cursed as he heaved himself onto his feet and brushed his hands off. He sighed as he drew his mind, once again, back to the present. He looked up at the stars and felt an odd sense of eternal peace. It was his body's way of preparing him for the looming struggles ahead. He didn't know if he would live or die, he didn't know if Davenport would live or die, he didn't know if Bradley would live or die, and he didn't know if the Brassy Gats would live or die. He didn't know anything, and it scared him. The unknown dragged his soul to the darkness, the supreme palace of unknowing. The baleful calm made the hairs on Alistair's neck stand, yet still he pushed onward. The degree of necessity trumped the degree of dread. Alistair knew he had to fight—and win—this war for his Brassy Gats, for his brothers, especially Colburn. Trouble loomed on the horizon, and Alistair marched forward toward his inevitable fate.

CHAPTER 10

Buildings came into view. The distant sound of crashing waves muted the faint tread of Alistair's feet. The soles of his feet cried for a break, and his arches ached. He didn't walk quickly for two reasons: He didn't want to be seen close to Bradley, and two, he didn't have any reason to make it to Conwy before daybreak. Yet, he arrived in the darkness. Hints of the sun began to show itself, but there was still no substantial light. The back line of houses began to get closer and closer, and all Alistair did was mindlessly walk forward. He didn't, nor couldn't, think of his past, his present, or his future. He walked a straight line with, for the first time, no thoughts. There wasn't anything Alistair could think about, as he had no idea where to start. Perhaps he could let his mind settle on the rare calm, or perhaps he should force his mind awake and alert. Instead, however, he opted to shut it down, let his legs walk without demand from his brain but rather with necessity from his soul.

"Halt!"

Alistair heard someone, but with his brain asleep, he marched forward.

"Freeze or I'll shoot!"

Alistair still kept his hands shoved into his pockets and his head down, like a moving statue.

"Sir, you have three seconds to identify yourself or I'll shoot."

Alistair still walked, his soul ill-equipped to listen and comply with demands other than its own.

"Sir!" The man cocked his gun.

"Do we have a problem here, Arthur?" called a voice from the open window of the building closest to Alistair.

"Oh, yes, Mr. Jameson. There's a man out here not listening to me." Alistair recoiled as his brain exploded to life. Flinching backward, he looked up. He was staring down the barrel of a rifle, standing right next to Conwy's outermost building.

"Ally! Stand down, Arthur. Ally, what are you doing?"

Alistair filled with happiness as he heard the voice of his youngest brother. To him, Davenport was still just a little kid, a naive soul in need of Alistair to be his guiding figure, to be his brother.

"Davy." Alistair huffed as his brother disappeared from the window and emerged from the door. Alistair took a dizzying step forward and collapsed into Davenport's arms. He was exhausted. His trek from the train had taken longer than it needed to, and it had drained his energy. He hadn't eaten anything substantial in days, and it was coming at a cost.

"Ally, are you all right?"

"Yes, yes. Just tired. It's been a long day."

"Come. I've had a horse saddled here for hours, waiting for you. We have a lot to talk about."

"We do indeed." Alistair cleared his throat and steadied himself on his own two feet.

"Have this." Davenport offered a half-eaten sandwich to Alistair, who humbly took it and wolfed it down. His stomach, tired from growling, sprang to life with the hint of food.

"There's more at home. Well, the temporary home now."

Alistair nodded and brushed the crumbs off his suit. He and Davenport walked around the old farmhouse, and Alistair saw one horse and some other equine animal standing next to it.

Alistair furrowed his brow and pointed to the creature. "What's that?"

"A mule."

"Why?"

"I won't ride a horse so long as Rouge is alive."

Alistair rolled his eyes and gingerly waltzed over to the horse. It wasn't as majestic as Atlas, nor was it a stealthy black. Alistair couldn't tell for sure, but he thought it had a gray pelt.

"Her name is River."

Alistair nodded, ran his hand down her mane, and mounted her. He and Davenport began their journey to the center of Conwy. As the sun began to rise over the trees, he noticed River was, in fact, gray. Not the color he liked, but he was too tired to be complaining about the color of a horse's pelt. This horse was so insignificant to his operations, he couldn't care about it. Too much was at stake to worry about minuscule details. The sun finally rose high enough to warm Alistair. His neck soaked up the heat of the rays and he welcomed the shine of day. Finally, Alistair and Davenport reached the heart of Conwy. The normally bustling fishing population was quiet. There were no fishermen getting ready to go out for a long day's work or returning home from their night at sea, and there were no vendors out on the street selling fresh fish. The welcoming charm of Conwy was replaced with the current hushed atmosphere of Burford. Alistair knew he brought it here. He brought war to Conwy and forced the locals into their homes, for fear of getting shot. The two brothers rode to the stables, counterintuitively next to the docks, and dismounted. There were no ordinary horses in the stable; instead, there were draft horses. Barely anyone in Conwy had a car; the citizens held on to tradition. Only two horses here were trail horses, one was River and the other one was missing. Alistair smiled as he knew that meant Bradley had taken the other older horse.

"This way." Davenport led Alistair out of the stables. Alistair felt a little bit of anger bubble up in his stomach. He knew his way around Conwy, and he didn't like being bossed around. The pair walked toward Conwy Castle, a fortification built in the 1280s.

Alistair always marveled at its beauty, strength, and longevity. The castle had been well preserved, and Alistair was certain Davenport already stationed troops in the castle just like their ancestors thousands of years ago. Bloody war after bloody war, and yet humanity still resorts to fights. Alistair was disappointed he was going to fight, but he knew there was no other way.

"All right, Ally. I've got men at every entrance to Conwy, like you suggested, in defensive positions. But I have only ten men inside, should the Snappy Kings infiltrate. Where's Brad?"

"Only ten?"

"Only half of the men Brad sent arrived."

"Why?"

Davenport shrugged his shoulders. "I don't know."

"You've done well, Davy. We're pressed for men and time."

"Speaking of men, where's our brother?"

"He's in the enemy camp."

"What?"

"He's going to try to gain their trust."

"Before they attack?"

"We don't know when they'll attack."

"Presumably in a matter of hours."

"Maybe Brad's presence will throw them off. That's what we've got to hope for."

Davenport opened a crate hidden under a pile of hay. "Here, take this." He tossed Alistair a rifle. Alistair grabbed it and felt the life instantly drain from his fingers. Alistair was a veteran, and he knew the soldier within his soul couldn't fade away. His soul, like Colburn, was an old soldier that would never die.

"Feels weird, eh?"

"Yeah," Alistair murmured. He cleared his throat and slumped the rifle over his shoulder. He was trained for this, almost as if the world knew Alistair's life depended on the victory of war not once, but twice.

"How many times do you have to repent before the weight of guilt disappears?"

"Repent?" Alistair chuckled. "We're all sinners."

"Not like me."

"We're headed to war, people will die. I've killed people, too, Davy."

"Not like I did." Davenport looked up into Alistair's eyes, and Alistair's heart skipped a beat when he realized his brother's eyes were glossy, as if he wanted to cry.

"No?"

"No."

"I know the tunnels were rough, but the trenches weren't happy days. I've seen men gunned down around me, I've been shot and nearly killed, I've gunned down men, and I've led men to their deaths."

"And I've been stabbed, I've been slashed, I've been beaten, I've been bitten, but I've done more stabbing, more slashing, more beating, more biting than has been dealt to me. You don't know what happened under the trenches, Ally." Davenport sniffled.

"Now isn't the time to think about this." Alistair laid his hand on his youngest brother's shoulder. "We may have to fight."

"I don't want my memoires to die with me. People need to know the terrors from war so they won't do it again."

"We're fighting again."

"Not in trenches and not under trenches."

"War is war."

"It's a good thing war is so disastrous, or, because of human nature, we'd be drawn to it."

Alistair nodded. Davenport's words hung in his ears. They were a perfect embodiment of humanity's devastating self-protective measures.

"You ready for this, Ally?"

"No, but ready or not, here it comes."

"O, that a man might know the end of this day's business ere it come! But it sufficeth that the day will end, and then the end is known."

"What is it with Shakespeare?"

"He writes art. His works speak volumes just sitting on the

shelf. What is the meaning of life if there's nothing enjoyable?"

"Huh." Alistair chuckled and shook his head. "Devoid of meaning."

"Exactly."

"Mr. Jameson! Mr. Jameson, a man approaches on horseback!"

"Battle stations!" Davenport commanded, and the men jumped up from their relaxed positions and aimed their rifles dead ahead. Echoes of "battle stations" bounced through each section of the men on guard.

"Ally, get down!"

Alistair, suddenly switching back to his soldier soul, grabbed his weapon and aimed it at the approaching horse. He could see his brother's rifle was aimed at the rider himself. He braced for the first shots of war.

Bang! Bullets flew all around Alistair, and gunshots tore through his ears. With each shell casing that hit the ground, Alistair flinched. He sometimes accompanied his father on hunting trips, but he wasn't accustomed to the persistent sounds of gunfire, nor was he accustomed to shooting at people. Alistair had never been more scared in his life. Beside him, he could see Bradley and Colburn quiver, too, and the three brothers felt their hearts give out with every squeeze of the trigger. Alistair could never get used to this, nor did he ever want to get used to it. Nothing was natural despite being surrounded by a wall of dirt. While physically close, he couldn't have been spiritually further from the natural realm even if he tried. He was the closest to humanity's Achilles' heel: fear. Alistair was terrified, a fright he feared would never leave him. He was stuck in an endless loop of fearing death and fearing fear. His rifle swayed left to right, and Alistair had no way to know, mainly because his eyes were closed, if he was hitting his targets. But judging by the cries of death, he was sure some of his bullets succeeded, because the Germans were running straight toward his trench, and it was hard for him to miss.

When the sound of his comrades' guns ceased, Alistair took his finger off the trigger and forced his eyes open. What greeted him was a sight he could never forget. Images of carnage, blood, flesh, and dying men ingrained themselves in his fragile eyes. He stepped down from the ledge of the trench and collapsed against a wall. His whole body trembled in a fashion he thought only earthquakes could. A ringing suffocated his ears and fogged his brain. He took short, rapid breaths and felt unsteady on his feet. Unable to stand, he dropped to his knees, sweating uncontrollably, yet he still felt dizzy. The blood traveled through his ears, and his chest threatened to burst with the pressure of his rapidly beating heart. He didn't know how long he had been on his knees before Colburn's face, or at least he thought it was Colburn, popped up in front of him. Muffled shouts came from somewhere close to Alistair, but he couldn't comprehend where. He began choking on his own saliva, and he reached for his throat. Alistair's mind replayed the same thought over and over again: *I'm going to die.* He was convinced he was going to slump to the ground dead, and the terror that engulfed his soul offered no room for hope.

"Alistair." A calm voice called his name. Alistair didn't know who was speaking, nor where the person was calling from. The man's voice sounded like an echo, and it left Alistair shaking harder. His limbs felt numb, and he couldn't move now.

"Alistair?" Again, the man called out to him. Alistair didn't know how long he had been choking against the trench wall. Was it thirty seconds or thirty minutes?

"Ally?" It was a new voice, a voice Alistair's petrified soul knew. But still his brain couldn't comprehend what was happening.

"Ally?"

Finally his brain caught up, and he recognized Colburn, who reached out gently and cradled either side of Alistair's head. Almost instantly, Alistair's face warmed up, and his body ceased shaking. He still felt lightheaded and weak, but his breathing slowed, and Alistair collected his thoughts. He could swallow and not spit it back up, and he looked up to meet his brother's concerned stare.

"Colburn—"

"Easy, Ally, breathe. You're okay, Ally. You're okay."

Alistair half-heartedly nodded and weakly reached out and rested his hands on Colburn's arms.

"Come on, brother, stand."

Alistair grunted as Colburn pulled him up. The numbness in his limbs was slowly fading, and with each breath, he felt the feeling return. He leaned heavily on Colburn as the pair began walking toward the medics.

"What's wrong with him?"

"Sir"—Colburn quickly saluted—"he needs water." The medic looked Alistair up and down. There was no blood on his uniform, at least not his own, and physically he seemed fine.

"He's fine," the medic grumbled and turned around.

At that moment, Alistair realized he was the older brother. He should be the sane one; he should be the one comforting his younger brothers.

"Where's Brad?"

"Shhh, he's over there."

Stubbornly, Alistair pushed off Colburn and took two steps toward Bradley before tripping on seemingly nothing and falling. Alistair wiped his hands on his uniform. His own feet had betrayed him. Colburn bent down and helped Alistair to his feet. Alistair whined as Colburn wrapped his arm around his waist.

"One step at a time, Ally."

Alistair reluctantly nodded. He shoved Colburn away again, but this time he didn't fall. He walked toward Bradley, who appeared unharmed, and embraced his brother in a hug.

"What's wrong, Ally?"

"Nothing, Brad. Just wanted to make sure you're okay."

Bradley sighed. "No one is okay."

"They are." Alistair signaled to their superiors. While all of the young and first-time soldiers were vulnerable to shell shock, the older officers seemed unharmed by death. Alistair was jealous.

"No, they're losing bits of humanity to pretend to be unaffected by war."

Alistair rolled his eyes. He wanted to be a superior officer one day so he could see the dead and not flinch. Alistair's heart wept because he knew soldiers that suffer from shell shock don't reach higher positions, or at least he assumed.

Colburn came up behind Alistair and walked over next to Bradley. "Whatever happens, we have each other. Jameson brothers for life." Colburn reached forward and drew his two older brothers into a hug. Alistair and Bradley repeated what Colburn said before falling silent. For what seemed like ages, the brothers didn't move; they simply rejoiced in each other's company.

"Battle positions! Let's roll, an unknown group of five men are approaching!" The brothers sprang out of their peaceful hug. Alistair wasn't scared anymore, or his soul tried desperately not to let his brain know the fear that stirred in his belly. He hated his rifle; the rifle made his fingers blacken with agony. He looked up at his general, awaiting further command. The general started morsing the men and, to Alistair's surprise, let out a sigh of relief.

"They are French."

Alistair smiled, as he knew what command came next.

"Hold your fire!" Davenport shouted.

Alistair shook his head and lowered his rifle.

"Ally, I've called out that command five times. Why didn't you stand up?"

"Sorry, Davy, my mind wasn't in the present."

"You can't win a simultaneous battle in the present and the past."

Alistair nodded. He knew Davenport was right. Alistair could never hope to win if he was constantly stuck in the past. Davenport stood up and wiped the dust and hay off his suit. Alistair rose slowly and did the same. He was worried, not about his safety directly, but about losing. He felt guilty; the Brassy Gats could never win if Alistair's past drained his attention and diverted his energy to events long gone. He just wished there was a way he could forget his struggles. Almost instantly, Alistair regretted that thought. It was naive to think his world would be better without his pain. His pain shaped him, made him who he was today. From the pain comes the character.

"You coming, Ally?"

"Where?"

"To the gates of Conwy; we have a visitor, remember?"

"Oh, right, sorry."

"You must really be out of it, eh?" Davenport chuckled.

"Why?"

"You're joking, right?"

Alistair shrugged. Davenport chuckled as the two brothers retraced their steps back toward the stable. Alistair felt ashamed and embarrassed, as if he had let his brother down. He should be more alert and focused. For the first time, his body stopped its pointless battle against fatigue, and Alistair was hit with a massive wave of exhaustion. He just wanted to sleep, and he knew a solid night's sleep would make him feel better. But he had work to do, and he couldn't sleep until it was done.

"We almost fired at you." Davenport chuckled, talking to the man on horseback.

Alistair whipped around and realized his brother had stopped and begun walking left, toward a man on horseback. Alistair felt a massive weight being lifted off his shoulders when he saw who was mounted on the old trail horse: Bradley.

CHAPTER 11

Alistair fumbled with the letter in his hands. He wished Bradley could've stayed longer, but Bradley was hesitant to be seen near his brothers. Alistair frowned and read the letter from Bradley over and over again. He'd already read it four or five times, and the language Bradley used was straightforward and simplistic.

"Ally, come on." Alistair lifted his head and rose from the chair in the parlor. Davenport stood in the kitchen, cooking a meal that Alistair assumed was the first thing he'd cooked since he was six. It smelled both good and bad, but Alistair's stomach didn't care, as he was starving.

"Come on, Ally. That letter isn't going to change."

Alistair grumbled as he walked over to the kitchen. How much was Alistair willing to sacrifice for Conwy?

"Hungry?"

Alistair nodded and slumped into a kitchen chair. The wood pushed against his back and forced his delicate soul to bend. He didn't want to think about Conwy anymore. In some sense, Alistair was ready to give up.

"Ally, you're the oldest here. We need you to be sane and functioning in order to secure a victory."

"How can you ignore this?"

"Because I have to."

"No, you don't."

"We need at least one functioning brother in charge." Davenport scooped some pasta into a bowl and placed it in front of Alistair and slid a fork across the table. Alistair grabbed the fork and wolfed down the pasta. The flavorless sauce added nothing but a watery texture to the already soft pasta, but Alistair didn't care; it was food. He eyed Davenport for more. Davenport sighed and dished out more. Alistair responded by promptly consuming it.

"This pasta is not good."

Davenport chuckled.

"It's terrible." Alistair joked.

"I can't do this on my own, Ally. I need you. I was underground the entire time. You're the man that rose from soldier to lieutenant in a matter of months. You led your platoon to numerous victories and saved your comrades' lives time after time. I struggle to understand why I'm the one with the gallantry medals."

"You're the one who singlehandedly knocked out an entire section of the German fortification."

"I'm the one that killed Colburn."

"Not this again, Davy. You saved Brad!"

"At the price of our other brother. Do you know how hard that was? I had Colburn's blood on my ankles, a reminder of the life I didn't save."

"And Bradley had your flesh on his arms, a reminder of the life that saved him."

Davenport drew a deep breath. Both brothers were in no state to lead a force against a larger one. Alistair breathed deeply, too, and he walked over and embraced his brother in a silent hug. Neither Alistair nor Davenport said a thing, but they didn't need words to suffocate the sufferings of each other, at least temporarily. The despondency from the current atmosphere lifted, allowing pure air to flood the room and shove the agony to the corners. Nature tried desperately to fix the wounds humanity inflicted on itself, but some wounds are too great. The pains from war, no matter how hard anyone tries, will always scar the mind and plague the soul. Healing, however, is a product of vulnerability, and humanity shies away from vulnerability. Only when humanity lets itself be weak can the whole world pick itself up and enter a state of happiness. Alistair knew he needed vulnerability, but he didn't have the strength to accept it.

Alistair breathed deeply and gently pushed away from his brother. "Davy, we need to regroup."

"Says the man who hasn't been present all day. You can't win if your eyes are clogged with visions from the past."

"And you can't live with the guilt you let wrap its greedy hands around your neck. Colburn's death is no one's fault but the Germans."

"The past is in the past."

"Colburn's death is the past."

"No, Ally. I live and breathe his death. Every morning, I wake up and wonder, what if I saved both of them? What if I had tackled Colburn into Bradley? What if I had tried harder to save him?"

"You need to move on." Davenport nodded. "Okay, Davy? Let's move on."

Davenport sighed and cleared his throat. Alistair scratched his neck and grunted. Davenport dragged his feet along the floor as he slid over to the table where the letter from Bradley lay.

"This letter is the most clear one I've ever read."

"Maybe there's some hidden meaning? Brad is cunning, perhaps there's a code in there somewhere."

"Yes, he is cunning, and as such, he wouldn't leave a code in a very important message that must be comprehended instantly."

"This is a huge sacrifice. We can't."

"We have to."

Alistair sighed and angrily fluffed his hair. He knew Davenport was right, but it was a hard pill to swallow. If the Snappy Kings caught wind of their plan, England would hear of the name Crail, not Burford.

"Mr. Jameson!" Alistair and Davenport turned their heads.

"Mr. Jameson! Urgent call from Burford!"

Alistair and Davenport both shot toward the door. A man Alistair didn't recognize held the receiver of the phone in his hand. Neither brother had heard the phone ring.

"Wilcot! For whom?" Davenport asked.

Wilcot Randy. Alistair remembered him.

"Mr. Bradley Jameson. A woman by the name of Ms. Beckingham is calling."

Alistair looked over at Davenport, puzzled. He stepped forward to accept the phone for Bradley. He was confused as to why she was calling.

"For you, Mr. Bradley."

"I'm Alistair, Bradley isn't here." Wilcot apologized and handed the phone to Alistair.

"What do you want, Ms. Beckingham?"

"Bradley?"

"No." Alistair clenched his jaw. He didn't like anyone hurting his brothers.

"Alistair?"

"Yes."

"Where's my Bradley?"

"Your Bradley? Loretta, you abandoned him and fled to Canada. He is not, nor ever was, your Bradley." Alistair heard a commotion behind him. Davenport had risen from the chair he slouched in and was walking toward him. Alistair remembered that Davenport didn't know Bradley's wife had taken off and left, with all his money, to Canada. She broke Bradley's heart, and although Bradley didn't lose his mind, Alistair knew his brother was still in pain. She had no right calling, and Alistair was determined to make Loretta realize the fault in her cowardly flight.

"Loretta?" Davenport whispered. Alistair shushed him with his hand.

"I was so ignorant, and I shouldn't have left."

"Damn right. And you shouldn't be calling, you broke my brother's heart and I will never forgive you for that."

"Please, Alistair, listen to me. There's something he needs to know. Where is he?"

"Unavailable."

"Why was I told he would be in Conwy? I called our—his—home in Burford, but the operator told me I could reach him here."

"He's unavailable."

"Alistair, I get you're trying to protect him, but I need to speak with him."

"What's going on, Ally?" Davenport stepped up and shook Alistair's shoulder. Alistair brushed his brother's hand off.

"Bradley is unavailable."

"Look, Alistair, I realize I made a mistake. But Bradley is technically my husband."

"By law but not by heart."

Loretta sighed, and Alistair flared his nostrils. She had abandoned him; she deserved to suffer the consequences.

"Let me speak to him," she whimpered.

Alistair didn't want to, nor physically could, let her speak to Bradley.

"At least deliver him a message?"

Alistair grumbled. "Fine."

Loretta took a deep breath and her voice trembled, undoubtedly from regret. "I'm pregnant."

Alistair fell silent. He was both furious and relieved; she had to come back now.

"I want to come back."

"Where's the money?"

"That's what you care about, Alistair? The money? I'm carrying Bradley's child, and all you care about is the money?"

"I could've had you arrested."

"Then why didn't you?"

Alistair grumbled. Davenport whined, upset about being left out. "Bradley told me not to."

"Then why are you protecting him, Alistair? He's a grown man, he doesn't need his brother to look after him!"

Alistair was taken aback. He didn't know a world in which he didn't protect his brothers. He always protected his brothers. It was in his blood.

Alistair stopped in his tracks. His platoon did the same, and no one uttered a word. Alistair looked over his shoulder and signaled for Bradley and Colburn to come closer. His two brothers carefully walked next to him.

"What's going on?" Colburn asked.

"Shhh, listen," Alistair commanded.

Bradley and Colburn stopped talking and looked around. The sounds of rotary engines roared in the distance, but with each second, they sounded like they were getting closer.

Colburn looked to the sky. "Planes?"

"Yes," Alistair responded dryly.

"That's not good."

"Do we have anti-aircraft guns?"

"We have one with limited ammo."

Alistair sighed. His platoon had been deployed on a top-secret mission behind enemy lines. They had one goal: Drive the Germans toward the British main forces. The only way to do that, Alistair and his superiors determined, was to fire from behind, forcing the Germans to either die or retreat farther from their homeland. It was the only way to trap them. Of course, their plan had limited chances of success, as the Germans could very easily be in trenches now. The only reason Alistair and his men were sent was because reconnaissance revealed the Germans here hadn't built trenches. Now they were faced with an unexpected challenge; aircraft engines roared in the distance, barreling full speed toward Alistair and his men. No one should have known they were here.

"Set it up."

"What?"

"Set it up, Brad." Alistair knew this was risky, but if these airplanes were, in fact, German, Alistair and his small platoon needed to knock as many as they could out of the sky. Bradley scurried off to the sole anti-aircraft gun and began setting it up.

"How do we know they're German?" Colburn asked.

"They're approaching from the south," Alistair answered. "That's their occupied land."

Colburn looked up to the sky. Alistair did the same, and he felt his heart skip a beat; the aircraft came into view. Alistair grabbed his binoculars and attempted to identify the origin of the planes. To his dismay, he saw the Iron Cross. "They're German."

Alistair looked around. His men were walking at the edge of a small woods, and thinking fast, he ordered them to take cover. The men did as they were told. Alistair couldn't shake the thought that these fighter planes were heading to his comrades in the trenches. He whirled his head around and eyed his men. Various degrees of fear spread on their faces.

"Brad! Come here." Alistair knew Bradley had the best shot on the anti-aircraft guns. "Roll the artillery to me."

Bradley nodded, and he and Colburn jumped forward, dragging the gun with them. His men benefited from shooting these planes down, but his comrades did more.

"Shoot them down."

"That'll give away our position."

"Shoot them down, Brad." Alistair stood behind Bradley as he aimed the artillery up. He took three steps back, afraid of the recoil, and held his breath. They had three shells left, and there were ten planes. In order for this to be successful, Bradley needed to hit every shot. Alistair didn't dare breathe as his brother aimed the weapon at the unsuspecting aircraft and fired. The first shell loudly crashed out of the artillery and flew through the air. Everyone held their breath as they awaited the sound of impact. *Bam!* There it was. The sound of turmoil exploded from the air as the first plane began an emergency descent. The second and the third shells followed in suit; three shells, three direct hits. Bradley had done it. Alistair sighed and let himself walk over to the other men, and they celebrated their victory as the remaining seven planes took immediate U-turns and stormed back toward their base. Their only problem now was that the Germans knew they were there.

"Let's go, Brad. Leave it, it'll only slow us down."

"Yes, Ally." Bradley let go of the anti-aircraft artillery, and the platoon emerged from the woods, hastily making their way toward the Germans. All Alistair had to ensure he was going the right way was a somewhat accurate map and a compass. The rest was up to fate.

"Colburn?" Alistair turned and searched for his brother.

"Yes?" Colburn came jogging up from behind Alistair.

"Is Brad okay?" Alistair glanced in Bradley's direction. Bradley walked with his head down, keeping a quick pace. "You know how . . . these kinds of things affect him."

"Yeah."

Alistair looked at Bradley again. Bradley had a hard time dealing with plane crashes. Indeed, it was Bradley who had been shot down in a plane, a plane he wasn't supposed to be in. Bradley was the sole survivor in that plane crash.

"You did the right thing, Ally. You aren't always going to be there to protect Brad."

"What?" Alistair spaced out, thinking about that moment he had failed Bradley as a brother.

"You can't always protect him." Colburn's words were right, but they left a sour taste in Alistair's mouth. Colburn reached out and put his hand on his brother's shoulder. "You can't always protect him."

"You can't always protect him."

Alistair snapped his head up as he heard not Colburn's voice but Loretta's. He was disappointed; he wished the voice at the end of the line was Colburn.

"I know." Alistair reached for the back of his neck and scratched it. He didn't want to talk anymore, not even to Davenport. Sighing, he thrust the phone in Davenport's direction and stormed away. Davenport shouted for Alistair to come back, but he didn't turn around. He was upset with the world, and he wanted to go home. Part of him lost his fighting spirit, but he remembered that when the spirit dies, so do the chances of victory. He couldn't do anything to jeopardize their already bleak chances. Alistair returned to the kitchen and picked up the note from Bradley. He spun it around in his hands again, trying to find any fault with it. In the other room he heard Davenport hang up and shuffle quickly to him.

"She left him?"

"Yes."

"Why didn't you tell me?"

"What was the point? She was gone, and Brad didn't want to add another problem to the mix."

"He trusts me, right?"

"With his life, Davy. We all do. You've saved many. You're a hero. If not the world's, at least your our hero." Davenport glowed. Alistair smiled; his brother's happiness meant the world to him. "If we're going to fight, let's do this right. No more moping around, no more worrying about bygones, and no more conversations with the outside world," Alistair declared. He switched on lieutenant mode and grabbed his rifle that lay on the armchair. Davenport did the same.

"Speaking of bygones—"

"Yes, I know." Alistair unfolded the letter he had put in his pocket. "This is something that has to happen in order for us to win."

Davenport nodded as Alistair opened a drawer and stuffed the letter inside. This was it, the dawn of a new era. War was coming, and it was Bradley who was going to suffer the first consequences. Alistair felt guilty that it wouldn't be him who would endure the pains of war first, but in the letter Bradley wrote, one thing was clear: Bradley needed to prove he was loyal to the

Snappy Kings, and they knew just the way. It would serve as a permanent reminder of Bradley's sacrifice for his brothers. Alistair was proud of Bradley's dedication and bravery and knew it was what needed to be done, but he shuddered at the thought of it.

Bradley was to be branded.

CHAPTER 12

Alistair and Davenport marched forward in unison. Their boots trod equally, and every sound was perfectly in sync. The two brothers were a force to be reckoned with. They walked to the walls of the castle and stopped. Alistair looked at Davenport and nodded.

"Men!" Davenport shouted. He turned and eyed the fragile city of Conwy. "Men! Today we fight! We fight for Conwy, this city. We fight not only for our survival, but for our families!" Cries from the various soldiers rang out, and Alistair felt a sudden burst of newfound hope. He kept his mouth shut, wary that Dirkson had men listening. Davy continued, "My wife is pregnant: Today I fight for the three of us! I fight for my brothers, Alistair, Bradley, and our dearly departed Colburn."

"For Colburn!" the others shouted.

Alistair smiled; his brother's name lived on. Everyone knew the importance that Colburn's name carried. Everyone who knew Colburn suffered from his death. *Old soldiers never die.*

"For Colburn," Alistair whispered.

"Old soldiers never die."

Alistair whipped around. Father Romano approached on horseback. He didn't expect the Father to come; no one had even told him they were going to fight.

"Father?" Alistair took three steps forward.

"I called Bradley, but his operator told me I could reach him here. Then I knew."

Alistair nodded and helped the Father off his horse. Father Romano's calming presence was much needed.

"Who do you fight for?" Davenport cried and opened his arms, inviting the soldiers to share.

"For my son!" one cheered.

"For my wife!" said another.

"For me!"

"For my parents!"

"For my nieces and nephews!"

"We all fight for someone! We may be outnumbered, outgunned, and less prepared, but we have more of a fighting spirit than they ever will! We cannot die, because our spirits are high! This ends today: Dirkson, Eastaughffe, and Cromwell will soon be distant memories of the past. No one will hear the name Snappy Kings anymore, only Brassy Gats!" Davenport proudly cried. The soldiers erupted in a glorious cheer. Alistair felt his soul rise from the depths of despair and fly, full force, toward the heights of hope. He felt united with his old soldier spirit, and these soldiers were the vessel transporting him back to a unique cacophony of brotherhood and death. This time, however, he was confident there would be no earth-shattering deaths. But he needed to be wary of this confidence; too much and it became cockiness. Cocky is just another word for suicide.

"It's now or never," Alistair whispered. He felt Father Romano's silent prayers.

"All right, men! We have limited information as to our enemies' whereabouts, but should they try to approach, they'll be seen! Fear not! We are a band of brothers, of friends! Victory is inevitable."

Alistair turned his head in Davenport's direction. His brother was getting cocky. Victory was not inevitable. Davenport instantly understood Alistair's glare.

"But remember, we can't win if we don't try! Optimistically, victory is forthcoming, but we must remember we can't be woefully optimistic or surely we'll be blinded." Davenport turned and mouthed *You happy?* to Alistair, then continued, "But don't forget: Unity is stronger than division. We shall fight, and God dammit, we shall win!" The men erupted into a glorious chant. There was no containing the fighting spirit that rose from the fire in Conwy's belly.

Davenport signaled with his hand, and the men dispersed and assumed their battle-ready positions. Alistair and the Father walked over to Davenport, both feeling out of place.

"What now, Davy?"

"We wait. Hello, Father." Davenport reached out and shook the Father's hand. Alistair knew his brother was overjoyed to see Father Romano. He held a powerfully calming presence everywhere he went. He wasn't the calm before the storm, he was the calm within the storm.

"Hold your fire!" Alistair shouted. This was his first command, and his men were young, untrained, and impatient. They fired their guns prematurely and inaccurately. Alistair was disgusted by his men's lack of respect. They didn't see him as their superior but, rather, their inferior. Alistair was young, too, as young as some of his callow soldiers. But where Alistair had poise, his men were hotheaded. He couldn't deal with these young soldiers; he feared they'd kill him.

"I said hold your fire!" Alistair was pissed. His men continued to fire, aiming at the hidden enemy. Not only could they not see what they were firing at, but they were giving away their position.

"Listen to your superior."

Alistair whipped around and saw Father Romano emerge from the safety of the shadows. Alistair barely knew the Father, but he was already grateful to have him deployed with him. For the most part, Alistair only heard bad things about Father Romano, like that he refused to touch a gun, would walk around the trenches in only his cassock, and only ate the scraps. Alistair, however, viewed those things as good: A real man of honor doesn't go against his morals for the sake of violence.

"Thank you, Father Romano."

"Just doing my job, sir."

"Call me Alistair."

"All right, Alistair. I heard you have three younger brothers?"

"Yes." Alistair scanned the horizon. His men had ceased their useless firing and awaited further command. There was no reason for them to react unless in defensive measures, as their main goal was reconnaissance.

"They aren't here?"

"No." Alistair grimaced. He had been pulled away from Bradley and Colburn to lead this sorry excuse of soldiers. He wanted out, and he wanted to be with his brothers.

"Request a transfer."

"I've tried."

"Turn these men around, and then your superiors will see your skill."

Alistair hesitated. He knew not to get his hopes up, but he would do anything to be with his brothers. The only thing he had no control over was Davenport. He couldn't magically bring Davenport aboveground, nor could he ever expect to see his youngest brother again. He knew the tunnelers died, and they died at a rapid pace. He feared his brother would become a statistic.

The sound of gunfire roared to life, and Alistair whipped his head around and saw Germans approaching from the south. He looked down at his three men who were supposed to be keeping watch on the south side, and they were laughing, smoking a cigarette, and playing some game in the dirt. Alistair was furious. He needed to do something drastic to get his useless men in line. He unholstered his pistol and fired it straight up. All the men flinched and looked up at Alistair.

"Having fun down there? This is war! There is no time for fun and games. Look with your eyes at what's coming! See them? See the

Germans? What do you three think you're doing?" The three men looked down, unable to make eye contact with Alistair. "I asked you a question! So either you respond, or there will be consequences!" None of them responded. Alistair clenched his fists, furious with the soldiers in front of him.

"Very well." Alistair turned and stormed over to a small trunk that lay tucked into the dirt. He grabbed a white flag from within it and stomped over to the three men.

"Get up and wave this flag!"

"What?"

"You heard me! Wave this damn flag!"

"But—"

"You three have been useless. If you were smart, you would've seen them coming! In fact, all of you are so disobedient, disrespectful, and cowardly that you've been telling me all along you want to surrender. So now, either you get up and wave the white flag, or you all get up off your asses and work! We are at war! Every move that you make—or don't make—has dire consequences. So what will it be? Because next time you don't listen to me, I'm forcing one of you at gunpoint to wave this cowardly flag!" Alistair flared his nostrils.

One of the men, Private Scott, grabbed the white flag and threw it to the ground. "Sir." He saluted.

The others gawked but refused to salute.

"Scott, go stand by Father Romano, the rest of you, the fate of us all lies in your hands."

Scott scurried behind Alistair and next to the Father, and then, on cue, the approaching Germans opened fire. The bullets flew over Alistair's head, but he didn't flinch. He looked each man in the eye, greeting all of them with his icy-cold stare. He wasn't going to fire back, or move at all, until each and every one of his soldiers pledged their loyalty to him. He needed them to understand the severity of the situation. The Germans continued to fire, yet Alistair refused to move. He could hear the Germans shouting now, meaning they were close and ready to rush Alistair and his men. Finally, the men moved.

"Sir." One by one, the men took a step forward and saluted. Alistair nodded his head. He waited for all the men in front of him to salute and hold it. The Germans were getting closer, so Alistair didn't have much time.

"Battle stations! Grab those guns and fire! Double time, let's go!" Alistair commanded. The men scrambled to their weapons and fired at the oncoming Germans, who were totally taken by surprise and were gunned down easily. It was a victory on two fronts for Alistair; he'd defeated a small German platoon, and he gained the respect he deserved. Now he was almost certain he could see his brothers once again.

"Good job, Alistair." The Father shook Alistair's hand. Alistair smiled warmly and walked toward his men, some shaking from the carnage they had caused.

"Well done. And now that you all have proved to me you are capable of respect, I expect it constantly. Understood?"

The men nodded. "Yes, sir."

Alistair nodded and told the soldiers how proud he was. He stepped out of the trenches, alone, and went to find the wounded Germans. He didn't want anything but information from them.

"Sir!" Alistair turned and was amazed to see all of his men emerge from the trenches.

"We couldn't let you go alone, sir," another called. "In case any wounded Germans try to shoot."

Alistair's soul glowed: These men, however inexperienced, rose to the challenge. His bond switched instantly to a fatherly one, despite their being close in age.

"Thank you."

"Of course, sir." The men heard shots of war far off in the distance, but Alistair had won one battle today.

Bang! Alistair jumped backward. He looked all around him and saw Davenport grab the rifle from over his shoulder and rush toward the north side of the castle. Alistair did the same and followed his brother. They both feared the same thing.

"It came from the north!" Davenport cried while sprinting.

"Who fired it?"

"I don't know!" The two brothers rushed up the stairs, two at a time, toward the northern outpost. Alistair swiveled his head, looking for evidence of gunshots, but couldn't see any. With every desperate step toward their men stationed on the north side, he felt his stomach sink. The only good thing was he heard only one gunshot. There wasn't any return fire, no shouts, and no cries. If it was indeed a war-hungry shot, it was tactical. Alistair feared he had underestimated the Snappy Kings.

"See anything, Davy?" Alistair and Davenport ran in a single-file line.

"Nothing!" Alistair felt his stomach spring to life and awaken his nerves. It was a feeling he first felt as an inexperienced soldier, not a trained lieutenant. This time, his livelihood was on the line, and he didn't want to lose everything. Not to mention, his brother's life was on the line. Bradley was swimming in the acid of the beast's belly and had already been burned. Alistair shuddered in an attempt to clear his mind from Bradley's branding. Then Davenport stopped suddenly, and Alistair, unable to stop himself, ran into his brother's back.

"What's wrong?"

Davenport didn't say a word.

"Davy?" Alistair stepped around his brother and saw the same thing Davenport saw. Alistair's heart sank and his anger skyrocketed. Firing only one strategic shot had been their enemy's plan. The Snappy Kings made their message loud and clear. There was no going back now. In front of them lay one of their own, Pete Alexi, lying dead with a single bullet wound in his chest. The Snappy Kings were on the prowl, and they were hungry for blood.

The first shot of war had been fired.

CHAPTER 13

This was it, there was no turning back. Alistair looked up at his brother, who was unfazed, and nodded.

"Welcome to war, brother." Alistair slapped his brother on the back.

"This is nothing."

"Stay aboveground, Davy." Davenport nodded and trotted forward. He walked with a balanced nonchalance. Somehow Davenport was able to merge humanity's confusion with nature's clarity. Underground, he was somehow stripped of what made him human and superficially filled with natural qualities. Aboveground, however, he was stripped of natural qualities and pumped full of human qualities. Alistair preferred his brother's humanity to his brother's naturality.

Alistair swept Davenport out of his mind as his brother turned the corner and walked out of sight. He turned and hurried back the way he had come, ready to relay the information to the middlemen, who transferred information from the north, south, east, and west positions. More importantly, he was rushing to prepare the ten men stationed in the heart of Conwy and Father Romano. The only message that could reach them was a verbal one. There was no way, Alistair felt, that he could get information to those men in such a risky manner as Morse code, which the enemy could intercept. He knew the consequences of poor choices, and he wasn't about to make the same mistake twice.

"Father!" Alistair picked up the pace, running down the corridor and jumping down the stairs. Father Romano came jogging up halfway.

"It's happening, Father. Alexi is dead—a single bullet to the chest."

"Why Alexi?"

"To make a point, I assume. Frank!" Alistair called out for the middleman Ernest Frank.

"Is Alexi special in any way?" Father Romano asked.

"Not that I know. Davy might."

"He was alone?"

"Yes, Father, I can't talk about this right now. Frank!"

Frank came into view, running full speed toward Alistair.

"Alistair, listen," Father Romano continued. "Someone knew that Alexi would be alone."

"Sir?" Frank slowed and awaited command.

Father Romano tried to position himself between Alistair and Frank. "Alistair, we've got a bigger problem. Stand down, Frank."

Frank looked at Father Romano, then back to Alistair, puzzled.

"Father Romano, these are my men. I command them—"

"All due respect, Alistair, you can't tell him anything."

Alistair was livid. The Father had no training, no experience, and no authority. He had no right telling Alistair nor his men what to do.

"Father Romano! Get back into the house, these are my men. This is my war, not yours."

"Alistair, please listen to me."

"Should I go or stay, sir?"

Alistair brought his hands to his face in an attempt to calm himself.

"Stay."

"Go."

Father Romano and Alistair answered at the same time. Frank looked around widely, unsure of what was happening. Alistair's eyes bore into Father Romano's skull, but Father Romano refused to give in. Alistair noted how perfectly still the Father stood, not even quivering under the weight of Alistair's chilling stare. He knew any second now, the Father would yield to his stare, but the Father's resistance made Alistair question if he should listen to what the Father had to say. Alistair sighed and turned to Frank. "Go."

"Yes, sir." Frank saluted and ran back toward his safe spot, right in the heart of Conwy.

"Thank you, Alistair."

"Don't thank me." Alistair pinched the bridge of his nose and shivered. "Why, Father, why?"

"Someone knew Alexi was going to be alone. No way that was a lucky shot."

Alistair nodded his head. Father Romano paused, and Alistair signaled for him to continue.

"Now you and Davenport have sprinted in opposite directions; you're split up. Someone knew that killing Alexi would cut off Davenport and the north defense from the rest."

"Inside man," Alistair grumbled. These were the hardest to catch, the hardest to predict, and the hardest to reason with.

"Exactly."

"And if I told Frank, it would mean, assuming the mole isn't in the north defense, that he would know Davenport and I were divided and the traitor would open fire."

"Yes."

"Stay here. I'm going to go get Davenport." Alistair turned and began to rush off toward the north defense, but the second he did, he heard a bloodcurdling sound.

Alistair tried to push himself up off the ground. His head rang and his arm lay limp and useless. He looked around and tried to gather a sense of what had just happened. He was young and he was terrified. He turned his head in either direction, scanning for Bradley and Colburn. He saw Bradley pull himself up onto all fours and stumble toward Colburn, who lay on his side, not moving. Alistair could hear his own breath as he struggled to heave himself up and rush to the aid of his fallen brother. Finally, he managed to collect himself enough to stand. He took one small step, then another, then another. He felt little pain except for the burning in his lungs from the inhalation of smoke. His main problem lay crumpled in front of him.

"Colburn!" Alistair fell to his knees as he cradled his unconscious brother's head. The dampness on his legs made him glance down. To his horror, he was kneeling in a pool of his brother's blood.

"He's bleeding, Brad!"

Bradley lowered himself down and tore open Colburn's uniform. Blood gushed from a gash extending from Colburn's hip to his rib cage.

"Medic!" Alistair yelled as he ripped the sleeve off Colburn's uniform and desperately shoved it into the massive wound to stop the bleeding.

"What's wrong with your arm?" Bradley asked.

Alistair looked at his arm and realized it dangled, nearly detached. "Dislocated." He turned his attention back to his still unconscious brother. Bradley got up and stumbled over to Alistair.

"What are you doing?" Alistair was livid. Bradley needed to be helping Colburn or he would surely die.

"Don't move. This will only hurt a little." Bradley knelt next to Alistair and reached for his arm.

Alistair flinched away. "What are you doing?"

"Popping your arm back in place. Calm down, Ally." Alistair leaned away from Bradley, but Bradley's long arms shot forward and grabbed his arm. Alistair yelped from the sudden burst of pain as Bradley maneuvered his arm and pushed hard. Alistair cried and tried to push Bradley away. He felt his bone rub up against his socket, and he bit down so hard, his tongue began to bleed. Then he both heard and felt a pop; his arm was back in place. The pain subsided into an ache, and both Alistair and Bradley shifted their focus back to Colburn.

"Medic!" Alistair shouted, angered that no doctors had rushed to his brother's aid. Alistair and Bradley couldn't control the bleeding and Colburn's breaths became shallow and slow. Alistair's breaths, however, were short and fast; he was terrified.

"Medic!" Alistair shouted again. He feared his brother's death.

"Medic!"

"Ally! Calm down, no medic is coming."

"Why? Our brother is dying!"

"Because"—Bradley pointed behind Alistair—"the medic is dead." Alistair whipped his head around. Sure enough, the medic lay sprawled out on the ground, arms spread unnaturally wide, and his legs, what was left of them, were bleeding horrifically. Alistair felt his stomach churn and his eyes froze in agony. He stumbled forward to the medic and put his hand on the medic's chest; there was no heartbeat. Alistair turned back to Bradley and shook his head. He shot up like a rocket and screamed. Only then was he able to see the horrible carnage—bodies, limbs, and dying men sprawled in front of him. Behind him, the injured were picking themselves up and then collapsing again when they saw what lay in front of them. Alistair grabbed his stomach and fell onto his knees.

"Ally!"

Alistair looked up towards Bradley. "Brad?"

"He's conscious!"

Alistair stood up and sprinted to his brothers. He still wasn't sure if this was a nightmare or a hellish reality.

"Colburn?"

"Ally," Colburn coughed, "am I dying?"

"Shhh, no, Colburn." Alistair reached forward and stroked Colburn's face. Colburn began to cough violently, spitting up blood. Alistair felt his heart race as he worried Colburn would choke on his own blood.

"Brad, should we sit him up?"

"We can't, this wound is too big."

Alistair looked at his brother and realized he was watching the life drain from him. Then he heard the sound of men, lots of men. Alistair looked up, covered in his brother's blood, and saw at least a hundred British men running toward them. He shot up and began sprinting toward them.

"Help, please help. My brother is dying." Alistair collapsed into the arms of one of the soldiers.

"What happened?"

Alistair took a few deep breaths and pushed away from the support of his comrade. "My brother is dying, help." Alistair pointed toward Bradley and Colburn, who had once again fallen unconscious.

"Where's the medic?"

"Dead."

"What happened?"

"I—I don't know." Alistair put his hands on his head as he tried to remember what had happened. "We were walking along normally. Then there was a lot of shouting and—"

"You don't look so good, sit down."

Alistair did as he was instructed. He looked up at the man talking to him. He had two blond curly strands of hair that fell free of his helmet.

"My brother is dying, please help." Alistair struggled to breathe as he pointed back toward Colburn and Bradley.

"Yes, you said that. What's your name?"

"Alistair Jameson."

"Alistair? My name is Tobias Marlee."

"Tobias? Tobias, please help, my brother is dying."

"Look"—Tobias pointed toward Bradley and Colburn—"he's getting medical attention." Alistair looked, and sure enough, Colburn had three men around him, dressing the wound and carefully loading him onto a stretcher. Alistair let out a sigh of relief and breathed deeply. Bradley was also getting some medical attention on his leg. Alistair was the most unharmed.

"Thank you." Alistair took Tobias's hand as Tobias helped him up.

"Drink." Tobias held his water bottle out for Alistair to take. Alistair took it and gratefully chugged the remaining water.

"Thank you."

"What happened here?"

"Tobias, please don't go." Alistair clung to Tobias's arm. Even though both of his brothers were receiving the necessary medical attention, Alistair didn't want to be alone.

"I'm not. What happened, Alistair?"

Alistair closed his eyes as he thought back to what had happened. Suddenly, Alistair opened his eyes.

"I remember."

An explosion rocked Conwy. Alistair flinched backward and stopped dead in his tracks. He looked up and his heart froze; the explosion had come from the north side. He bounced up and sprinted like a madman toward the source of the sound.

"Davy!" Alistair desperately cried his brother's name, but he didn't get a response. He heard someone else come sprinting behind him and assumed it was Father Romano.

"Davy!" Alistair tried again, but to no avail. Then suddenly, he came to a complete stop. Fire was sneaking its way along the flora growing in between the stone, but that wasn't the real threat—a massive chunk had been taken out of the castle. Alistair was now separated from Davenport.

"Davy!" Alistair called again, fearing the silence.

"Ally?" Davenport moaned. Alistair could feel the pain Davenport was in, but at least he was alive. Alistair peered into the smoke and debris but couldn't make out much. His heart raced with the idea of losing another brother, and he knew he needed to get to Davenport.

"Alistair." Alistair felt a hand rest on his shoulder. He didn't need to turn around to know who was behind him.

"Father."

"Fret not, Alistair. Davenport is in good hands." Alistair turned to face Father Romano.

"Which horse did you ride here, Father?"

"My horse?"

"Yes."

"My brilliant young mare, Macey. She's an excellent horse." Alistair shot forward, sprinting back toward the center of Conwy.

"Where are you going?"

"Trust me, Father!" Alistair didn't turn around. He felt silent tears run their silent course down his broken face. He didn't hear the Father's footsteps following him. He approached the stairs and leaped down them, falling down instead of landing. He picked himself up, feeling no pain.

"Alistair!" Alistair heard someone calling his name, but he didn't care. Finally, he reached the stables. Looking around, he spotted the Father's mare still tacked. She was a dark bay Oldenburg—Alistair could tell just from looking at her—which meant she was a skilled and powerful jumper.

"All right, Macey." He reached out and stroked the horse's muzzle. He traced her powerful neck muscles with his hand before he grabbed her mane and mounted her. She was not pleased. Alistair cursed as the horse spooked, neighing loudly. She reared hard and fast, trying to throw Alistair off. Alistair leaned forward and held on. He had experience with spirited horses, but he didn't have the time to deal with this.

"Easy girl, easy." He stroked her neck, and she continued to rear.

"Come on, shhh." Macey continued to rear, upset with Alistair's presence. Sighing, he hopped off. Macey calmed down, but her eyes were wide open, her nose flaring. Alistair grabbed her reins and led her out of the stable. Ideally, he would build a rapport with her and learn her special traits, but now he didn't have the time. He needed to get to Davenport before it was too late.

"All right, Macey, easy." Alistair stroked her muzzle again and she knickered. "I need you to cooperate. Just this one time, all right? Can you do that for me?" He kept stroking her as he slowly walked to her side and gently mounted her. This time she didn't spook.

"Good girl." He urged her forward, and Macey broke into a sprint. She was a fast horse, her speed matching the intensity of Alistair's desperation. He led her back up the steps and through the narrow corridor of the castle before the deep hole loomed into view. Father Romano seemed unsettled by his horse's presence.

"No! Alistair, no. She may not make it."

"If she can't, we'll both die."

"No!" The Father protested, but Alistair didn't care. He kept the brilliant mare galloping right toward the hole. By now, the smoke had risen well above the castle, and he could just barely see through the dust. The sight he saw terrified him: three men lay on the ground not moving, two men were trying to pick themselves up, and one man collapsed dead center. Alistair had no way of knowing which was his brother, but he desperately hoped he wasn't dead. The dire situation not only threatened to end the war before his side could fire a shot, but it threatened Alistair's sanity. The world was playing tricks on his mind now, testing him. First Colburn died, and now Bradley was out of view and Davenport in distress. Alistair dug his heels harder into Macey's belly. She whined at the increase of pressure, but she seemed to understand Alistair's raw desolation.

"Alistair, stop!"

"No, Father Romano." Alistair was letting his agony guide his actions. He hoped that he wouldn't regret this decision.

"Please."

"This is war, Father, war. The risk is worth the reward."

"No, Alistair, you could die."

"Davy may already be dead."

"Davenport!" The Father shouted toward the injured and dead men that made up the north outpost, but no one reacted.

"Davenport!" He tried again. Alistair's chest began to tighten as again no one reacted. Alistair could feel the death flowing over the hole and snaking its way into his heart. He prayed that his brother's soul remained firmly planted on Earth.

"Come on, girl." He forced Macey closer and closer toward the gaping gash in the castle. Her hooves bounced on and off the stone, thundering ever closer to the wound. Alistair kept his eyes focused on the men in front of him, not daring to look down. He didn't want to see the hole that could be his death. If Macey refused to jump, he'd be thrown off and right into the mouth of the hole. If Macey jumped and failed to reach the other side, they'd both fall down. And if Macey jumped and reached the other side, Alistair would be reunited with his brother.

"Alistair, it's not too late to stop her."

"Yes it is, Father Romano, yes it is." Alistair's fear increased tenfold, and he could feel Macey's do the same. He tried to reassure her that all would be fine, but he didn't believe that himself. And yet, Alistair urged her on, as he had no other options. He needed to get to his brother, the whole of the Brassy Gats relied on Alistair and Davenport being together. Alistair knew he was putting his life in the hands of a horse he barely knew. All his life, he found himself relying on a horse or his judgment. Right now, he relied on both. Alistair took a deep breath, as he and Macey were one stride away from the edge of the hole. He prayed she'd make it and he prayed Davenport was alive. He held his breath as Macey decided whether or not to jump. His heart went still as he felt Macey's decision. He closed his eyes and let nature determine humanity's fate.

Macey's legs pushed off the ground as she leaped toward Davenport.

CHAPTER 14

The wind blew Alistair's hair behind his face. He welcomed the air as it whistled in and out of his ears, ringing his brain and forcing his eyes open. Taken by a fit of curiosity, he looked down. The sight beneath him slowed time. Debris from the mighty castle littered the ground. There was a degree of anger and fear bound together by a single flight. Alistair felt the rage within him rise; he needed to find the man responsible for this. He had allowed someone into his operation who was willing to betray his comrades. Betrayal is the ultimate form of cowardice. Then Alistair felt Macey collide with the ground, and his distress dissipated. Macey had made it. Alistair pulled back on the reins, bringing her to a complete stop within seconds.

"Davy!" Alistair jumped off the uneasy horse and rushed to the first man he saw. Blood trickled from the downed man and stained his shoes. Bending down, Alistair turned the man over. His eyes were glazed and glossy, his lips pale, and the warmth fleeting; he was dead. Alistair rubbed his eyes and felt the stress within him rise. Already they had two men dead, most likely more. But Alistair could selfishly take pleasure in the fact that this man was not Davenport—his brother might still be alive.

"Ally?" Alistair whipped around and saw Davenport rise to his feet and stumble toward him.

"Davy!" Alistair jumped up and sprinted to his brother, hugging him close.

"What happened, Ally?"

"An explosion. Are you hurt?" Alistair pushed away from his brother and gasped. Davenport's head oozed blood from a gash right above his temple. Alistair tightened his grip on his brother, as he felt him shaking.

"My head hurts."

"Sit." Alistair guided his brother to his knees. "Don't move, okay?" Davenport nodded. Alistair reached out and tore a bit of Davenport's already ripped shirt and carefully wrapped it around his brother's head. He had to stop the bleeding. Around them, men groaned. Alistair sighed as he realized he'd have to help the other men too.

"Can you stay here, Davy?"

"Yes."

"Lie down, okay?" Alistair got up and almost tripped on a body. Kneeling, he gently reached out and closed the dead man's eyes. Rifling through the man's pockets, he found his tags: Charles Hanover. Alistair sighed. *I promised his mother he wouldn't be hurt.*

"Mrs. Hanover, this is a minor conflict." Alistair sighed. He hated lying, but he needed all the manpower he could muster. Charles had been instrumental in recruiting Bradley and Colburn to Alistair's platoon during the war, so he and Charles already had somewhat of a friendship.

"I'm an adult, Mother, I can make my own choices." Charles took three steps toward Alistair and Bradley before his mother stopped him and grabbed his arm. Alistair swayed on his feet, annoyed at the precious time they were wasting.

"Think about your younger sister, Charles. She hasn't been the same since your brothers were killed. How would she feel if she had no brothers?"

"Mother, please. Alistair saved my life on so many occasions, plus he's the one that gave us enough money to survive after the war. I owe him one."

"You don't owe him your life." His mother was close to tears.

"Ma'am, we'll return him to you safe and sound."

Reluctantly, she let go of her son. "Promise?"

"Promise," Alistair said calmly. Tearfully, Charles's mother hugged her son. Alistair smiled as he turned and waved, walking away with a new recruit.

I shouldn't have promised her. Alistair rose and floated over to the next man lying on his side. A massive chunk of shrapnel had bored itself into this man's chest, and Alistair knew he, too, was dead. He bent down and closed the man's eyes, like he had done with Charles. Likewise, he searched through this man's pockets until he found some identification. Roger Francois, a Frenchman. Alistair cursed, as he knew Roger was Davenport's friend. The two of them had tunneled side by side all throughout France. Davenport had even learned French so as to be able to talk with Roger, who spoke no English. After the war, Davenport taught Roger English. Alistair turned back and looked at his weakened brother, not sure if he should tell him about Roger's death. He spotted Roger's dog tags and carefully took one off his limp wrist.

"Davy?" Alistair took a few steps toward Davenport, still hesitant to tell him about his friend.

"Yeah?"

"I'm so sorry, but that blast killed Roger." Alistair held out Roger's dog tag. Davenport looked confused.

"Roger?"

"Yes."

"No." Davenport tried to stand but collapsed. Alistair rushed to his brother's side, bearing his brother's weight.

"Not Roger, he was a gentle soul."

"I'm sorry, Davy."

"Give me his dog tag." Alistair knelt next to his brother and gently placed Roger's tag in his hand. Davenport slid it on his wrist, rubbing it as he began to cry.

"He hated the tunnels."

"I'm sure everyone hated them—"

"No. He *hated* them. Sometimes after we finished he'd purposely collapse them."

"Isn't that dangerous?"

"He never killed anyone. Well, not that we know anyway."

"How'd you end up working with him?"

"Somme. The French needed help, and I was the best the British had to offer."

"Two gallantry medals."

"But at what cost?"

"No cost, you saved millions." Davenport smiled and looked up at Alistair. Alistair placed his hand behind Davenport's head, carefully supporting it. His wound was getting worse and his blood began to thicken.

"Am I dying?"

"No, Davy, no. Your head is cut, that's all. Come, let's get you help."

"There are others, right? How is everyone else?"

Alistair rose gently and turned around. Behind him, two men huddled behind some debris, shell-shocked. Alistair walked over to them.

"Get back! We'll shoot!" The two men drew their rifles.

"Stand down! It's me, Alistair Jameson."

Embarrassed, the two men lowered their guns. "Sorry, sir," the two mumbled.

Alistair reached out his hand and helped the men to their feet. They were both covered in blood, but it was not their own.

"It's okay, it's okay. What happened?"

"There was a gunshot. We all tensed up and rushed to our battle stations. Then Davenport came flying, shouting something about Alexi. Then he tripped over seemingly nothing. But when he got up, he looked terrified. He shouted for us all to get back and hide. No one could react quickly enough, and then there was an explosion."

Alistair felt the fear within him rise. The man who planted the bomb used a tripwire, meaning there could be other traps hidden in plain sight. "Then what?"

"Then the stone exploded and came crashing down and men were flung. Davenport himself was launched and hit the wall over there." The soldier pointed to a spot opposite where he was standing. "Hanover was violently thrown into the stone and bounced off, crashing down onto debris. Francois was hit with debris, and Marlee was—"

"Marlee?" Alistair whipped his head around and searched for his old friend. He saw him, lying on his side. Blood had pooled around his torso, and Alistair didn't know if he was dead or alive.

"Tobias!" he shouted and rushed to his wounded friend's side. Alistair put his hand on Tobias's chest and felt an extreme rush of joy as he could feel a heartbeat, albeit a weak one.

"Tobias?" Alistair didn't want to move Tobias. His body weight was already providing pressure on the wound, slowly stopping the flow of blood.

"Alistair?" Tobias opened his mouth and blood poured out. Alistair froze with fear. He knew his brother would make it, but he wasn't sure about Tobias.

"Father!" Alistair shouted and sprinted to the edge of the hole.

"Alistair! Is everything all right?"

"Two dead, three alive, one badly wounded. Davenport has a bad cut on his head, but he's conscious and stable right now."

"Can he be transported on Macey?"

"Too risky. Father, Tobias needs immediate medical attention or he'll surely die!"

"Who?"

"Tobias Marlee. Please, Father Romano, he needs help."

"Send one of the men by horseback." Alistair turned and dashed over to the two soldiers. They huddled together, both very distraught. Alistair tried to calm his breath as he squatted in front of them.

"Who are you?"

"Chris Engles, sir. Bradley recruited me."

"Charlie Morton, sir. Bradley recruited me too."

"Engles, Morton. Can either of you ride a horse?"

"No, sir, I've been afraid of horses all my life. My little sister fell off of one once. Now she can't move," Chris said. Charlie shot a worried glance at Alistair; clearly, Chris's story bothered him.

"I'm scared too," Charlie said.

Sighing, Alistair rose to his feet and dashed to his brother.

"Davy," Alistair said, gently shook his brother, "how do you feel?"

"Dizzy."

Alistair knew he couldn't make Davenport ride Macey, but he asked anyway. "You can't ride, can you?"

"No."

Alistair sighed. He couldn't go back on Macey, as he needed to calm the men down and tend to the wounded Davenport and Tobias.

"Father," Alistair shouted, "they're scared!"

"Davenport?"

"He's in no condition to ride!"

"I'll get help."

"How will they come?"

"I don't know."

"Tobias is dying!" Alistair turned away from the hole and rushed back to Tobias. Tobias was his best friend, the man who had stood with Alistair through thick and thin. He was there at Colburn's funeral, there the day Esme was born, and there when Alistair's wife died. Alistair couldn't let Tobias die.

"Come on, Tobias." Alistair felt tears threaten his facade of strength. "We can't win without you." Alistair held Tobias's hand firmly and sank forward, resting his head on Tobias's side.

"Alistair?"

"Shhh, Tobias, don't speak." He stroked Tobias's blond hair.

"Whatever happens, I want you to know that you"—Tobias broke into a coughing fit—"you're destined to do great things. Things high above this business. I bet you could be prime minister."

Alistair felt a tear burst free and glide down his face. "Tobias—"

"Alistair!"

Alistair didn't move; he couldn't move. He was watching the life drain from his best friend, and it froze him.

"Alistair! Come here!"

Alistair couldn't leave his weak friend.

"Go, Alistair," Tobias whispered.

Alistair nodded and slowly rose.

"Alistair!"

Alistair snapped his head around and backed away from Tobias. He shoved his hand into his eyes, trying to stop his tears.

"Alistair!"

"Coming, Father!" Alistair reached the hole and peered over, spotting the Father on the other side holding a long wooden plank.

"Take this." Father Romano put the plank down, stepped on the end, and slid the plank across. Alistair grabbed the other side and pulled. The plank was more than long enough to extend the diameter of the hole, but Alistair questioned its strength. He didn't know if it would support the weight of two men.

"Go get Tobias," Father Romano ordered.

Alistair nodded. Throwing off his jacket, he approached Tobias carefully. He reached out and tried to roll Tobias onto his back.

"What are you doing?"

"Getting you help."

"Can't you bring them to me?"

Alistair shook his head. The local Conwy doctor was in the middle of town. Alistair didn't trust anyone but the doctor. He couldn't risk the mole coming with the doctor and sabotaging poor Tobias, thereby killing him.

"You ready, Tobias?" Tobias nodded, and Alistair gently turned Tobias flat onto his back. He quickly wrapped Tobias's chest in his jacket and carefully lifted him, carrying Tobias to the edge of the hole. The whole time Tobias groaned in agony. Alistair couldn't bear to look at his friend; he was too afraid to see him die.

"You're okay, Tobias."

"I'm dying."

"No, no, you'll be okay." But Alistair wasn't sure he believed that.

"Fret not, Alistair. Everyone must die. If this is how I go, I will have lived a full life."

Alistair bit his lip in a last-ditch attempt to stop the tears from coming. Tobias began coughing, and Alistair worried he was choking on his own blood.

"Hang in there," Alistair whispered, barely audible to himself. He didn't fully know if he was talking to Tobias or himself. He took a deep breath and stepped onto the plank. It hissed and moaned with even the slightest amount of added weight.

"Careful, Alistair!" the Father shouted from across the hole. Alistair felt sweat collect on his forehead. "It's not going to hold your weight, Alistair!"

Alistair barely took three steps, and already he felt the plank warp underneath him and heard a little bit of cracking. "It has to!"

"Alistair, you have to turn back."

Alistair refused to turn around. He needed Tobias alive, so crossing the hole was a necessity.

"Alistair!"

Alistair looked down at Tobias. His eyes were closed, and the wound had begun to bleed heavily.

"Father, he needs to live!"

"If you step any farther, you'll both die."

"He needs medical attention immediately!"

"Turn back, I'll go get the doctor."

Alistair saw Father Romano turn and sprint back toward the center of Conwy. Alistair sighed and reluctantly turned around. He could feel the plank shake with every step he took, so he quickened his pace and stepped back onto the ground. He gently sank to his knees and carefully laid Tobias down. His heart dropped as he noticed Tobias's eyes were still closed.

"Tobias?" Alistair got no response. He felt the anger rise within his soul and the trauma of war rush into his heart. He had had men die in his arms before, but Tobias was different. Tobias was a friend, someone Alistair wrote to on a daily basis.

"Tobias?" Alistair tried again. He leaned forward and placed his ear on Tobias's chest. He was relieved to hear a faint heartbeat.

"Ally?"

Alistair turned. He suddenly felt embarrassed; he had been ignoring his youngest brother. No matter how loyal Alistair was to Tobias, his loyalty to Davenport was stronger.

"Davy." Alistair rose and made his way to his brother.

"Ally, you're covered in blood."

Alistair looked down. Indeed, blood had stained every stitch of white shirt. "It's not my blood."

"Tobias?"

Alistair nodded. "How are you feeling, Davy?"

"I can barely see."

Alistair drew in a sharp breath; he knew Davy feared the dark. He wrapped his arms around his distraught brother.

"It's okay, Davy."

"No, it's not! I need to see. A blind man is a dead man!"

"Shhh, it's okay, Davy. Deep breaths, can you do that for me?"

Davenport nodded.

Alistair could hear his brother whimpering, trying hard not to cry. "What do you hear? Name three things you hear."

"You . . ." Davenport's whimpering got quieter. ". . . a horse's breath, and water."

"Good, good. Now, what do you feel?"

"I feel stone."

"No, what do you feel?"

Davenport sat up straighter and squinted his eyes as he attempted to see something. "I feel—" Davenport hesitated. "I feel fear."

Alistair pulled Davenport into a hug; his brother's suffering seemed never-ending. It was only a matter of time before it killed Davenport.

"Mr. Jameson?"

Alistair looked up and saw the doctor, pacing around, trying to find a way to get over to the wounded.

"Doctor Matt." Alistair looked back at Davenport. "Doctor, can you cross?"

The doctor, carrying medical supplies in both his hands, took a few steps onto the plank. It creaked and groaned a little bit, but the doctor didn't weigh as much as Alistair and Tobias. The doctor pushed forward. "I believe so, sir."

"Then come, quickly. I've got one man dying, and my brother has a bad cut on his head." He heard the doctor scamper over the precarious plank. All the while, Macey paced back and forth, unsettled.

"Mr. Jameson," Doctor Matt said, kneeling next to Davenport, "what happened to him?"

"Go to Tobias first." Alistair pointed to where Tobias lay in a pool of his own blood. "He is dying." The doctor nodded and scurried off to Tobias.

"Go to him, Ally." Davenport collected himself and pushed away from his brother's embrace.

"No, Davy. You're my brother. I am not leaving you."

"I'm not dying."

"Davy, you're hurt. You can barely see. I know how you fear the darkness."

"I fear the absence of light, not the darkness."

"Same thing."

"No, Ally. That's where your view on the world is wholly pessimistic."

"And yours isn't?"

"No." Davenport turned away from Alistair. "Mine is realistic. Cynical when it's deemed necessary, hopeful the rest."

"You're never hopeful, Davy. You cling hard to the past, a chronic anger for things far out of your control."

"Mr. Jameson!" Alistair looked up and saw Doctor Matt waving him over. Alistair welcomed the break. The philosophical conversation with his wounded brother was too heavy for such desperate times. Alistair put his hand on his brother's shoulder and rushed over to Tobias and the doctor. He prayed his friend was still alive.

"Yes?"

The doctor looked up at Alistair, grief floating in his deep brown eyes.

"It's not looking good."

Alistair hung his head and bit on his lip. He needed Tobias. Tobias had guided him through the pangs of suffering, sufferings that his own brothers were too knee-deep in to be of any assistance. Tobias was lucky; he had lost no one. He had no brothers in the war, no best friends lost, and nobody's life in his own hands. Tobias had been spared a lot of the pain, but he, too, was damaged from the Great War. Now, Alistair's war threatened the life of his best friend.

"What happened?"

"The blast must've been close to him. He's got a massive cut deep into his chest, so deep I can see the very bottom of his rib cage. He needs to get to a hospital now if there's any chance of him surviving. His leg is also broken from the impact with the wall, but it's likely that's what saved his life. His leg absorbed the force of his collision with the wall, and if it hadn't, there's a good chance his chest would've absorbed it and he would've died instantly. You wrapped this wound in your jacket, right? That's done a great job at slowing the bleeding. Head up, Mr. Jameson, you've done all you could. But we need to get him to a hospital now, or he'll die. Unfortunately, the nearest one is in the next town over."

Tears blocked Alistair's ability to think. There was little hope for Tobias, and it dwindled with each coming second.

CHAPTER 15

Alistair could feel his heart race. There was nothing he could do to help his wounded friend. Tobias's life now rested dually in the hands of Doctor Matt and a higher fate. Alistair clutched his heart and looked up toward the sky. He felt abandoned. High above him, he felt the holy presence of his beloved brother. He reached up in a futile attempt to grab Colburn, but he knew there was nothing he could do to bring back his dead brother.

"Ally?"

Alistair turned his head and saw Davenport limping his way over to him.

"Davy! Don't move." Alistair swept the tears off his face. "I'll come to you."

"How is he?" Davenport asked. Alistair turned to where Tobias lay sprawled out. Doctor Matt had been working twice as hard to clean and dress the wounds, and he had blood all over his hands. Alistair turned back to Davenport and shook his head.

"I'm sorry, Ally." Davenport looked over Alistair's shoulder. "Is that him?"

Alistair turned and saw who Davenport was looking at: Roger Francois. He sighed and nodded.

"I'm sorry, Davy." Alistair looked at his brother's face. Davenport's face was pale, too pale. Alistair noticed that Davenport looked unsteady on his feet, as he swayed from right to left. Alistair reached out to support his brother, but Davenport swatted his hand away.

"Davy—"

"Take me to him, Ally."

Alistair put his brother's arm over his shoulder and guided him toward where Roger lay. Davenport didn't need help to collapse to his knees. Alistair knelt next to his brother, who didn't even try to stop the tears from coming. Alistair didn't think it appropriate to say anything, so he let his brother mourn in silence.

"I miss Brad," Davenport said after a while.

Alistair nodded. "Me too." He knew there was nothing he could do but wait for Bradley's return, just like all he could do was wait for someone to come and save Tobias.

"Alistair!"

Alistair shot his head up at the sound of Father Romano's voice, but he couldn't see him. He rushed to the edge of the hole and looked down, fearful Father Romano had fallen.

"Alistair!"

Alistair turned around. The Father's voice was coming from somewhere behind him. "Father?" Alistair looked around.

"Down here!"

Alistair rushed toward the edge of the castle and peered over. Sure enough, he saw Father Romano carrying a ladder.

"Father, get back! It's not safe! The Snappy Kings could be anywhere!"

"It's okay, Alistair, it is. If I die, it is because God has greater ideas for me. Lower Tobias down, and I'll ride to the next town over with him."

"Father, we need you. You keep morale high."

"Perhaps, but this is the only option to save your friend."

Alistair nodded and scurried back to the medic. "How stable is he?"

Doctor Matt looked up, startled by the urgency in Alistair's tone.

"Not at all stable. He keeps fading in and out of consciousness."

"If we wait for medical—"

"We can't wait, or he'll die."

Alistair bit his lip and turned his head away from Tobias. "Doctor, I know how we can get him help, but it's risky."

"Take the risk, he will certainly die if he stays here."

Alistair nodded and rushed back to the wall and shouted down to the Father. "Father! He's coming. Do you have the horse ready?" Alistair could hear the sound of a horse coming from below. Once again, nature's horses were helping humanity escape its problems.

"Yes, Alistair! Hurry, hurry."

Alistair nodded and rushed back to the doctor and Tobias.

"A horse—" Doctor Matt shot up and grabbed Alistair's shoulder. "He'll die."

Alistair shoved Doctor Matt's hand off and knelt down next to Tobias, who was still unconscious. "You said yourself he'll die if he stays put. Dress the wounds, he's being transported." Alistair turned and looked the doctor dead in the eyes. "And this is a direct order."

The doctor hesitated but bent down and carefully wrapped Tobias's wounds in more gauze. Even still, blood seeped through the new layers, immediately staining the gauze.

"If he dies, it's not my fault." Doctor Matt looked up at Alistair, visibly upset.

"No, doctor, it'll be mine."

The doctor nodded and gently carried the unconscious Tobias. "It's better that he's unconscious right now, otherwise this would be very painful and a whole lot harder."

Alistair nodded and carefully walked next to the doctor, who strongly clutched Tobias and cradled him close to his chest. The three of them approached the wall, and Alistair's anxiety increased tenfold.

"Father! The doctor is coming down with Tobias. Please be careful, doctor."

Doctor Matt looked up at Alistair, and Alistair was startled by how upset the doctor looked. "You don't need to tell me to be careful, I already know."

Alistair rolled his eyes. He didn't have time to worry about insulting people.

"Doctor? I'm ready for him now," called Father Romano.

Doctor Matt carefully swung one of his legs over the wall and settled it on the top of the long ladder.

"I'm holding it steady!"

"Wait!" Alistair turned and grabbed the first rifle he saw. "I'll spot you. No way in hell I'm letting anyone shoot you."

The doctor nodded and resumed his slow descent down the shaking ladder. Alistair kept his finger firmly on the trigger, swinging the gun around from right to left, scanning the land for any dangers. Now he had three lives resting on his protection, and he wasn't going to let any of them die, Tobias included.

Alistair looked down and saw the Father struggling to keep the ladder from shaking. "Careful!"

Doctor Matt struggled to make any progress down, as he risked either dropping Tobias or falling. Alistair looked behind him and saw Davenport sitting against the wall and gently holding Roger's cold hand in his palm. Sighing, he slumped the rifle over his shoulder and bent over the wall, grabbing onto the ladder to keep it stable. There was no way he could ask Davenport to either hold a rifle or hold the ladder.

"Thanks, Alistair."

Alistair watched as Doctor Matt began to descend again. Slowly, he dropped one rung at a time, not daring to go any faster than necessary.

"Is he still alive?" Alistair watched as the doctor stopped moving and gently placed his head on Tobias's chest.

"Yes!"

Alistair let out a tension-heavy sigh. He watched as the doctor reached the bottom of the ladder. Only then did Alistair let go and grab the rifle over his shoulder to support the trio at the bottom.

"Alistair! He's alive!"

Alistair looked over the edge and felt joy beginning to kindle his cold soul.

"We're leaving. Godspeed." Father Romano mounted one of the horses he had borrowed from the Conwy stable. Alistair held his breath as Doctor Matt and Father Romano carefully lifted Tobias and placed him in front of the Father. Alistair knew Tobias was in great hands. Father Romano was an amazing rider; he wouldn't let Tobias fall off.

"Godspeed, Father." Alistair watched as Father Romano saluted and turned the horse and galloped away. "Are you coming back up?" Alistair leaned forward and grabbed the top of the ladder to steady it for Doctor Matt.

"No, sir. I'm walking around."

Alistair nodded and turned back to his wounded brother.

"Sir?"

Alistair turned around and saw Chris walking toward him.

"Yes?"

"Can we cross the hole, sir?"

Alistair peered behind him and saw that the weak and cracking plank was still suspended across the gash in the Conwy Castle.

"Of course."

Chris and Charlie slowly and carefully made their way across the plank.

"Go with them, Ally. I'm fine."

"No way, Davy. I'm staying with you. We'll find a way to get you across."

"Alistair"—Alistair jerked his head back, taken aback by the firmness in Davenport's voice—"listen to me. If we hope to win, you're needed to lead our men. I am fine, Ally. I can't walk well, but I'm not dying. You've already saved Tobias, now go. There's no reason for you to stay here."

"I'm your brother, that's reason enough."

"No, that's stupid. Ally, I am fine, believe me. I've fought battles without you by my side."

"That's exactly why I can't leave you."

"You left Brad."

Alistair flinched. He missed Bradley with every inch of his heart. Bradley's position within the enemy camp, however, was vital to their hopes of winning.

"Davy, that's not fair. You and I both know he had to."

"You could've sent me, but instead you opted for Brad. Do you not trust me enough?"

"No!"

"Am I too hotheaded, too impulsive?"

"No—"

"Then what is it, huh?"

"Davenport, calm down! You know Conwy better than either of us. You know its weak points and its strong points. Your intelligence is more valuable here than out with the Snappy Kings. Let's not fight, okay? You're injured and we've got a city to win."

"Sorry, Ally. I don't know what came over me."

"It's—"

Alistair was cut off by the piercing sound of gunshots. He whipped his head around as his heart raced. The gunshots were coming from the south side, and this time there were multiple shots. This time, Alistair was certain these were the gunshots of war. He heard shouts, too, the barking of orders and the cries of pain.

"Go, Ally"—Alistair turned back to his brother and watched as Davenport shakily rose to his feet—"Godspeed."

Alistair looked at his brother, weak from his head trauma, and grabbed him close. The gunshots still rattled off in the distance, yet Alistair felt at peace holding his youngest brother close. He also felt strangely comforted by the fact that Davenport was far away from the fighting.

"Stay safe, Davy." Alistair signaled toward Macey, who looked startled by the loud gunshots. "Keep an eye on her."

"I will, and stay safe too."

Alistair turned and sprinted off to the hole before stopping abruptly. He turned his head to the sky and smiled before turning to face Davenport. "Old soldiers never die."

"Old soldiers never die."

Alistair nodded and looked down at the thin plank. He had to trust that the cracking wood would support him across the lethal hole. He took a deep breath and began to cross quickly. With every step he heard the wood creak and crack, but it held on, and Alistair crossed without falling. Not daring to look back at his brother, he took off toward the gunshots. He grabbed the rifle still flung over his shoulder and ran. As he approached the center of the castle, he saw Frank fast approaching.

"Sir! Gunshots reported on the south side."

"I can hear!" Alistair didn't bother to slow down.

"Sir! Two of ours are wounded, but not fatally. The bullets only grazed their arms, and they are getting medical attention right now. Unclear, but an estimated three of the enemies shot and one presumed dead."

"Anything else?"

"No, sir."

Alistair nodded and rushed up the stairs toward the south side, taking them two at a time. He turned the corner and noticed his men firing through the slots in the castle. Bullets crashed into the stone, some ricocheted back, and others broke straight through the castle's walls. Suddenly, something flew over the walls and landed inches in front of Alistair. He bent down and instantly knew what lay in front of him—a grenade.

"Grenade!" Alistair shouted and quickly grabbed it and threw it back over the castle walls. Unfortunately, it detonated midair, having no effect on the enemies below.

"Men, what's happening?"

"Well, sir, there's only about ten of them down there, but they've got a lot of ammunition and grenades."

"Only ten?"

"Yes, sir, there can't be more than fifteen."

Alistair dropped onto all fours and crawled to the edge of the wall. Carefully and slowly, he rose, with his back on the wall, and peered over his shoulder, down onto the men that were firing at him and his comrades. Sure enough, he counted twelve men but a whole pile of rifles.

"Twelve, but there are enough rifles down there for thirty people." Someone from below spotted Alistair and fired. Alistair dropped his rifle and rolled away from the wall and toward his comrades.

"Thirty? Why do they only have twelve?"

"I don't know."

"Maybe they don't have enough men?"

Alistair looked up at the man he was talking to, breathing heavily. "What's your name?"

"Henry Barclay, sir."

Alistair looked up and squinted at Barclay. He remembered that name. *Henry Barclay.*

"Get down!"

Alistair turned and jumped down, frightened by the sternness of the general's voice. This was only his second battle, and Alistair wasn't any less terrified than the first one. He looked to his left and saw Colburn focused on the approaching Germans. Alistair could hardly hold his rifle steady; Colburn, however, seemed remarkably calm. Alistair looked over his right shoulder and saw Bradley behind him, rifle swaying too. Suddenly, thunderous bullets erupted from both sides. Alistair grabbed his gun and fired straight, although he could barely see who he was firing at. Neither side was battle-ready, as they were both completely exposed. They were in a flat clearing surrounded by a forest, both sides hoping to relocate and dig a new trench.

"Colburn, what's happening?"

"We surprised each other, I guess. Just fire."

"I'm trying."

"If you don't shoot them, they'll shoot you."

"If you don't shoot them, they'll shoot you," Alistair muttered as he returned his focus back to the Germans. He kept repeating that phrase over and over again as he calmed his nerves and fired. His rifle soon stopped swaying and sweat stopped dripping. *If I don't shoot them, they'll shoot me.* Alistair realized that his fright was only counterproductive; if he wanted to win, he needed to live. The only way to live was to kill rather than be killed. That was his justification. Suddenly, Alistair spotted something flying in the distance and immediately took his hand off the trigger; the Germans were flying a white flag.

"Hold your fire!" General Davidson rose slowly, rifle still pointed dead ahead, and took a few steps toward the Germans. No Germans fired at him.

"Stand, men, stand!"

Alistair hopped up, relieved to hear Bradley grunt as he rose because that meant he was alive and unharmed. Alistair looked at Colburn, who kept his rifle pointed at the Germans. Alistair quickly did the same and noticed all his comrades held their weapons in the same way.

"Drop your weapons!" the general ordered the Germans. The German general shouted something in German, and all their soldiers rose with their hands up, although most remained on the ground, dead. Alistair looked around at his comrades and realized almost everyone stood up; only a few were dead or wounded.

"Get them."

Alistair and his comrades trotted forward, walking toward the surrendering Germans. Alistair had no clue what they were going to do with these Germans, as they were miles from the main forces that were still in the trenches. It would be counterproductive to return just to drop off only a few Germans.

"Wait, you ten"—General Davidson pointed at the men on his left—"go grab their weapons and food. The rest of you stay as you are."

Alistair nodded and kept his weapon pointed at the defenseless Germans. His arms were starting to get tired. The German resources were quickly collected, as there weren't that many.

"All right, stand down."

Shocked, Alistair hesitantly lowered his rifle. He looked at Colburn, who just shrugged.

"Let's go, we don't have any reason to capture them."

Alistair was taken aback by the general's kindness.

"Sir, we just killed more Germans than are left. Why spare them?"

Alistair spun around and was ashamed when he realized Bradley was challenging the general.

"I must be cruel to be kind."

Bradley nodded.

"Shakespeare, sir?" asked a comrade whom Alistair had never heard speak before.

"Yes, that's right." The general stepped towards the soldier who had just spoken. "What's your name, son?"

"Henry Barclay."

"Well done, Barclay. Let's move out!"

Alistair nodded and advanced forward with the rest of his comrades. Bradley came trotting up next to him, still embarrassed from challenging the general.

"It's fine, Brad."

Bradley nodded. Alistair turned to talk to Colburn, but he realized his brother wasn't next to him anymore. Frantically, he spotted him about two paces behind talking to Barclay.

"You read Shakespeare?" Colburn asked.

"Love him," Henry responded.

"Me too! My parents have a book of sonnets he wrote and I've read practically all of them."

"His sonnets are amazing." Alistair turned back toward Bradley, letting Colburn and Henry talk without his eavesdropping. Alistair smiled. Through the darkness of war, Colburn was going to make a lifelong friend, he was sure of it.

"Sir?"

Alistair returned to the present moment. "You're Colburn's friend, right?"

Barclay smiled warmly and dropped his head. "That's right, sir. He and I would talk about Shakespeare every night until, well, you know."

Alistair nodded. He cleared his throat and pushed Colburn out of his thoughts.

"You said maybe the Snappy Kings don't have enough men?"

Barclay nodded. "That's right, sir. That's why they have more rifles than men."

"No, that can't be possible. The Snappy Kings have been planning this out, they even hired Andrei Popov to kill me. They think I'm dead. They wouldn't be this careless. Something is wrong."

"What's wrong, sir?"

"It's almost like they want to distract us. They have enough guns to do the job without using up a lot of their men."

"Distract us?"

"Oh my god." Alistair jumped to his feet. "Davenport!" Alistair took off sprinting toward his wounded and defenseless brother. He felt his heart speed up, as he realized how exposed the north side was. This was the Snappy Kings' plan all along—separate Davenport from his men and kill him, thereby ending the war with minimal bloodshed. Shooting Alexi was meant to draw Davenport away from everyone else, and the explosion was meant either to kill him or cut him off from everyone else. Alistair clenched his teeth, as this meant someone from the north side was the traitor working for the Snappy Kings. He had to get to Davenport before Dirkson, Eastaughffe, or Cromwell could; he wasn't about to lose another brother.

Alistair flew past Frank, who called out his name multiple times, but Alistair didn't stop. Each panicked footstep bounced off the pavement and sent chills down his spine and into his heart. He was terrified that he wouldn't make it in time. His vision narrowed, and all he could see was what was right in front of him—the stairs up to the north side of the castle—yet he could feel the distance between him and his brother like it was a needle prick; it was an acute pain like no other. Alistair had been shot before, yet this pain burned more. This pain was ineffable, sharp to the point of intolerable. Alistair ascended the stairs like they were nothing. As he turned the corner, his heart stopped. Cromwell and Eastaughffe held back Davenport's arms as he kicked and pushed back. They were having a hard time controlling him, but there was something more powerful preventing Davenport from escaping their grasp: the gun Dirkson was aiming right at Davenport's heart.

"This whole silly operation of yours is over before it even has a chance to defend itself. You can meet your brothers now." Dirkson chuckled.

"Brothers?" Davenport questioned.

"Alistair and Colburn."

"Alcott, there's something you don't know."

"What would that be, Davenport?"

Alistair flew down the corridor and practically jumped across the plank. There was no way he'd let Dirkson kill his brother, no way. Alistair snarled and launched himself at Dirkson, tackling him to the ground and knocking the gun out of Dirkson's hand.

"Alistair is alive," Davenport said, chuckling.

Alistair's temper exploded, punching Dirkson so hard, his hand began to bleed. Dirkson struggled against Alistair, but he was no match for Alistair's anger. Alistair unloaded another punch square on Dirkson's face, breaking his nose and causing thick blood to drip from Dirkson's face. Alistair loaded for another hit, but he felt someone grab his wrist. Alistair turned around and met Eastaughffe's fist. He fell backward off of Dirkson and stumbled to his feet, grabbing at Eastaughffe's shirt. Cromwell was desperately trying to restrain Davenport, but Davenport was too strong, and Cromwell collapsed. Suddenly, the sound of a gunshot stopped all the fighting. Alistair's eyes darted to Dirkson, whose face dripped blood and whose nose ballooned and turned purple. He was again holding his gun.

"Enough! Frederick, Oliver, come here." Cromwell and

Eastaughffe trotted to Dirkson's side. "Alistair, what a pleasant surprise."

"The pleasure is all mine." Alistair spat.

"Popov—"

"Failed." Davenport snickered.

"Shhh, Davenport, the adults are talking."

"Don't you dare speak to my brother like that." Alistair took a threatening step forward. "Or does your face want more reconstructing?"

"I have the gun, Alistair."

"So did Popov."

"I have a gun too." Oliver Eastaughffe took a step forward and aimed his gun at Alistair's head. Alistair was not scared, or at least that's what he told himself.

"Me too." Frederick Cromwell took a step forward and aimed his gun at Davenport. Alistair cursed as he realized he had dropped his rifle back on the south side. He could still hear the gunshots from the other side.

"So the power really rests with us, doesn't it, Jameson brothers?"

"Looks can be deceiving, Alcott. You of all people should know that."

Dirkson laughed. "Alistair—" Dirkson was cut off by Macey's panicked nickering. "Dammit, shut up! Perhaps we should relocate. Down." Dirkson pointed his gun toward the edge of the castle.

Alistair looked at Davenport and nodded. Neither he nor Davenport had a gun, and there was nothing they could do but be compliant. He knew that not following Dirkson's demands could be a fatal mistake. He was terrified, but he had to pretend not to be.

"Get on with it! There's a ladder, so convenient."

Alistair audibly cursed as he realized he never removed the ladder from the side of the castle; this was on him. He put his hands up and walked over to the side, thrusting his leg over and placing it on the ladder below. Angrily, he began to descend, and Davenport followed suit, Tobias's blood still fresh on the ladder.

The two brothers began their humiliating trip down the ladder and out of the castle.

"Don't try to run, Alistair and Davenport, or I'll shoot you."

Alistair rolled his eyes; he wasn't planning on running. Running would be cowardly, and he was no coward.

"What are we going to do?" Davenport whispered.

"Try to stall," Alistair quietly responded.

"How?"

"By doing what they say."

"Ally, my head is killing me. I feel faint." Alistair looked up at Davenport worriedly.

"Hang in there, Davy." Alistair shuddered as he felt his foot touch the dirt below. He pushed off the ladder and eyed Dirkson. Alistair didn't break eye contact with Dirkson, but he could feel his hope fleeting.

He couldn't see any other outcome besides his and Davenport's deaths.

CHAPTER 16

Alistair could hear nothing but his own heart beating; the fear of death silenced everything else. There was nothing to save him now but time. Even that would only delay the process. Alistair was stuck toeing the line between wanting a quick end and delaying the process long enough to remember his life.

"Keep moving." Dirkson shoved Alistair in the back. Alistair clenched his fists. This wasn't how the battle was supposed to go. He had never been taken prisoner during the war. He looked at his brother, worried Davenport would collapse from the stress of death and his concussion, but Davenport looked calm. Alistair cocked his head, confused at his brother's composure.

"The tunnels change a man, Ally."

Alistair nodded, realizing Davenport had endured more stress than this. Davenport ventured to the darkness of death day after day, and Alistair had ventured only to the edge of that darkness. Alistair never forgot the day Davenport returned home from the war. His youngest brother was not the same man he had been before the war; Alistair wasn't even sure if he was a man. In order to be human, one must be alive. Alistair didn't know if his brother lived in the mortal realm anymore. He knew certain aspects of

Davenport's life kept him afloat—Rouge, Cordelia, his unborn child, his brothers—yet Colburn's death dragged him down beyond the living world. Alistair, on the other hand, had pulled men like Davenport from the firm grasp of agony. Only this time, there was no one to save him or Davenport. They were on their own, marching toward their inevitable deaths. Alistair never thought his death, or Davenport's, would come so soon.

"We'll be okay, Davy," Alistair whispered.

"The miserable have no other medicine but hope."

Alistair smiled faintly. Through the darkness, Davenport still found something to hold on to. Shakespeare, however unimportant to most, was essential to Davenport, Alistair saw that now. Shakespeare beguiled Davenport's woe, as it was Davenport's way of dealing with the grief.

"Keep moving!" Dirkson barked.

Alistair could still hear the gunshots ringing from the south side, yet he wasn't sure if anyone knew they were gone. Alistair shuddered. By the time anyone figured it out, it would be too late. Alistair never thought he feared death, but this time was different. He had a daughter to live for, sweet Esme, and brothers to protect. Alistair succumbed to man's tendency to fear the unknown—in this case, death.

"Here's good enough," Dirkson barked. Cromwell and Eastaughffe came to a stop, never lowering their guns aimed at Alistair and Davenport. Alistair could feel the sweat beginning to form, yet he refused to display his fear. Fear would make him weak, and Dirkson would exploit weakness.

"Alistair, I didn't think I'd get to kill you myself." Dirkson snickered.

"You don't have to." Alistair matched Dirkson's cold stare.

"I've been looking forward to killing Davenport, though."

Davenport shot his head up and snarled. "Why would that be, Alcott?"

"I'm a nice person, Davenport. I had a horse once, a wonderful mare, but she fell and broke her leg, so I shot her, you know, to put her out of her misery."

"What's your point?" Alistair hissed. He hated Dirkson's cockiness.

"My point is, I'd be putting you out of your misery, Davenport. The guilt you feel must be unbearable; after all, it is your fault Colburn is dead."

Alistair drew in a quick sharp breath. Davenport clenched his fists and pressed his lips into a thin line; Dirkson had struck a nerve. Alistair knew it wasn't Davenport's fault and that Dirkson was just trying to rile him up, and Davenport fell for it.

"I saved Brad."

"You saved the wrong brother, Davenport. Your dear Bradley is on our side. I branded him myself last night. I've never seen a man be branded so stoically."

Alistair shot a glance toward his brother. Davenport looked even paler than before, white as a sheet of paper. He swayed on his feet, his eyes full of despair. Alistair feared Davenport would do something stupid. He was struck by how similar Davenport looked to the first time he saw him after Colburn's agonizing death.

Alistair and Bradley turned to look at each other, neither brother saying a word. They slowly walked to the white fence of their childhood. The flowers in the garden were all wilted and dead, the grass unkempt, and the house looked run-down. Alistair could hear the faint whining of a horse, but that was all. Not even the birds sang.

"We did it, Ally."

Alistair reached out and grabbed his brother. They smiled for the first time in a long time.

"We won the war." Alistair took a deep breath. "It's good to be home." The air around his home felt oddly comforting. Even though his parents weren't always the kindest, he missed them dearly. They, too, weren't the same; the loss of a son weighed heavily on their souls.

"You ready?" Bradley asked.

Alistair nodded and gently placed his hand on the gate. He swung it open slowly, rejoicing in the peace and ease that accompanied it. At the same time, the door to the house flew open. Alistair and Bradley jerked their heads up and stopped dead in their tracks. Alistair felt memories of his childhood flood into his brain and nostalgia rise in his soul. Staring back at him was his father, who looked tired and weak.

"Alistair! Bradley!" He took off sprinting toward his sons. Alistair smiled big, as he'd never seen his father run before. He'd always been laid back, but now he ran with great speed. Alistair opened his arms and embraced his father, who had tears in his eyes.

"Father." Alistair choked on his words and let the warm, fatherly embrace cheer him up. He let his head settle in the groove of his father's neck and stayed there for what seemed like an eternity. Finally, Alistair stepped back and let Bradley feel the nirvana of home.

"Alistair!" Alistair looked up and saw his mother come flying out of the house. Her hair was wild and unkempt, her face drained from the hours of crying, and her back hunched from the countless days of constant worrying. Alistair rushed to his mother and hugged her close. She was frail and partially collapsed into his arms.

"You're so thin." She shuddered at Alistair's gaunt body. Alistair knew she was right, as proper meals were hard to come by. It was another reminder of the sacrifices he had made for his country.

"Bradley!" She pushed away from Alistair and rushed to Bradley's side. Bradley let go of their father and nestled his mother close. Alistair looked at his father as he stepped next to him.

"Welcome home, son."

Alistair smiled, unable to speak. He was too afraid to speak, too afraid that he would wake up. His father, sensing his fear, put his hands on Alistair's shoulders.

"It's all right, son. You're safe here."

Alistair nodded. He brushed the tears off his face and yawned. "Do you have tea?"

"Of course." His father gently led him away from the gate and toward the house. Alistair hesitated, eyeing the doorframe. He had done it, and now he was home. Turning, he saw Bradley and their mother following them. His heart sank as he remembered Colburn would never be able to return home.

"Come, son." His father pulled Alistair inside. Alistair was instantly hit with a wave of warm air, and he let his soul relax. He was home. He was alive. Most importantly, he was safe. Safe from physical threats, at least, as his terrifying memories already threatened to snake their way back to the forefront of his brain.

"I'll put some tea on."

Alistair nodded and walked to the kitchen. The house was just as he remembered it: Photos of him and his brothers lined the far wall, the kitchen still had the chipped wooden table and matching chairs, and the carpet still had the stain from Alistair dropping chocolate when he was seven.

"My boys," his mother said, tearing up, "where do I even start? I'm so happy you're home."

"We're glad to be home," Bradley responded.

"Where's Davenport?" their mother asked.

"He's coming."

"We're so proud of you, of all of you." Their mother reached out and stroked Alistair's face. Years of hard fighting had made his skin rough, and she was visibly shaken up by the firmness of his flesh.

"What did the Germans do to you?"

Alistair shot a glance at Bradley, and the two of them looked down.

"They shot us," Bradley said. "Slaughtered millions of us."

"My poor babies."

Alistair walked over to the kitchen chairs and slumped into one. He took off his shoes and let his head fall back.

"Here's some tea."

Alistair perked up and eagerly grabbed the tea from his father.

The sound of the fence gate opening and closing startled everyone. Alistair and Bradley leaped up and grabbed the rifles they had placed on the table. Then, in walked Davenport. Alistair held his breath as his brother froze at the door frame. He looked around, frightened. Alistair's heart burst as he realized how meek his brother was. He was no more than skin and bones, very pale, and very fearful. He swayed, unsteady on his feet, refusing to come inside.

"Davenport!" Their mother burst forward and wrapped her arms around him. He coughed at the impact and shrieked. He pushed her off and collapsed to the ground, eyes wide with terror. Alistair rushed toward his brother and knelt next to him.

"It's okay, Davy, it's okay. The war is over, this is our mother."

Davenport slowly turned and met Alistair's gaze.

"Mother?" He rose slowly as she nodded her head. He took three small steps forward and embraced her close.

"Am I home?"

"Yes." Their father joined in on the hug. Alistair retreated next to Bradley, both heartbroken at the sight of their terrified and weak brother.

"He'll never be the same again, will he?"

"We won't be the same either, Brad." Alistair looked at his brother and reached out and grabbed him close.

"We're home, Ally. We did it."

Alistair teared up again. Davenport jogged up to his brothers and silently joined their hug. Alistair smiled and let the breathing of his brothers remind him that they were alive. He didn't want to leave their embrace. Alistair could feel his misery fleeting every second he remained in his brothers' arms.

"We have tea." Their father came and placed his hands on Alistair's back.

Davenport shot his head up. "Tea?"

"Yes."

"May I?"

"Of course."

Davenport let go of his brothers and stumbled through the doorway. He instinctively grabbed his revolver as he turned the corner, all the while keeping a steadfast watch on the ceiling. Alistair's heart melted as he realized Davenport didn't feel safe in his own home. The Germans had taken away something that no one should have been capable of taking away. The idea of safety appeared to be fleeting in Davenport's mind.

"Davenport," his mother whispered, heartbroken by this baleful sight.

"Davenport," his father repeated, equally dejected. Davenport suddenly froze; the stress of fear was too much, and he swayed on his feet before lurching forward to catch himself on the wall.

Davenport collapsed. The thud from his brother's body snapped Alistair back to the present.

"Davy!" Alistair fell to his knees next to his brother.

"Ally," Davenport coughed, "I killed Colburn, didn't I? Maybe Alcott is right."

"No," Alistair whispered. "No, he's wrong. You didn't pull the trigger, the Germans did. The Germans killed our brother, not you. Don't ever forget that. Dirkson is just lying," Alistair hissed.

"He's weaker than we thought," Dirkson said with a maniacal smile. Cromwell and Eastaughffe chuckled.

Alistair shot to his feet. "My brother is stronger than you know! He won two gallantry medals—two! How many do you three have? None, none! What's your game plan, huh? Shoot us, God dammit, kill us! If you wanted to shoot us, you would've already done it, leaving our corpses in the castle for my men to find. So why haven't you?"

"Oh, Alistair." Dirkson chuckled. "We do have an audience." He signaled over his shoulder, and Alistair cursed. Approaching them were the Snappy Kings; every man who came to fight was fast approaching.

"Get up, Davy." Alistair knelt down to help his brother to his feet, but Dirkson fired his gun straight up.

"Let him get up by himself," Dirkson snarled.

"You're cruel, Alcott."

"I know." Dirkson shrugged, almost pleased with Alistair's accusation.

Alistair rolled his eyes and turned his attention back to his struggling brother. *Poor Davenport.* The explosion had already weakened him, and now Davenport was again confronted with Colburn's death while facing his own.

"Brave men." Cromwell spread his arms and welcomed the men who approached. "Here we have Alistair and Davenport Jameson!"

Alistair shuddered as the men erupted into a unified cheer.

Cromwell turned to Alistair. "Shhh, listen, you hear that?"

Alistair could indeed still hear the gunshots from the south side. He hoped no one had been killed, but right now he had his own life to worry about.

"Chain them," Dirkson ordered. Cromwell stepped back and aimed his gun at Alistair. Eastaughffe holstered his gun and grabbed two handcuffs he had in his trench coat pocket. The cold metal sent chills up Alistair's spine and despondency straight to his heart.

"Meet our newest prisoners, the leader of the Brassy Gats and his youngest brother!" Dirkson fired his gun straight up, and the others cheered. Through the cheering Alistair thought he could hear Bradley. He scanned the crowd. Sure enough, he spotted his brother, as he was the tallest man in the crowd. He towered over everyone. Bradley met Alistair's gaze, and Alistair could feel his heart break. He might never get the chance to say goodbye to Bradley.

Eastaughffe shoved Alistair, and he fell to the dirt, unable to brace himself because of the handcuffs. Dirt flooded into his mouth, but Alistair choked on embarrassment. He was humiliated. He had never been treated like this. Alistair peered back at Davenport, who was firmly looking down. Alistair knew Davenport's head was killing him, and he was probably throbbing with the same embarrassment. There was nothing Alistair could do but yield to the men wielding the guns.

Oliver Eastaughffe laughed as he retreated to Dirkson's side. "Bring the stake here!"

The crowd parted and three men emerged carrying a small

metal stake and hammers. They placed the stake in between Alistair and Davenport, and Alistair could hear a long chain snake its way to him. The sounds of hammers and chains formed the ultimate cacophony of despair, and Alistair thrust his body right and left in an attempt to right himself. He was able to get to his knees, but a hand kept Alistair from standing. He looked up and saw Eastaughffe loom over him. Alistair was all the more humiliated.

"These two are unlike any other prisoners we've had before, and as such, we want to give them some special treatment. With these chains and this stake, Alistair and Davenport will be chained out here for three days and three nights, the same as they did to our beloved Marcus!"

"For Marcus!"

Alistair cursed as he realized what was happening.

"Marcus?" Davenport whispered.

Alistair nodded. "Remember the butler I had who, about three years ago, tried to steal my daughter and take her to Dirkson?"

"Yes. He just disappeared after that."

"No, not quite." Alistair looked down, embarrassed. "I chained him up in the forest as a punishment. For three days and three nights I never gave him a second thought. Then afterward I went out there and shot him. The only reason Dirkson knows is I unknowingly told one of their spies."

"Jesus Christ, Ally. Why didn't you tell me?"

"Because I didn't know he was important. I thought he was just trying to make some quick cash."

"Have a taste of your own medicine, Alistair."

Alistair snarled. He knew he was going to die, but he refused to accept his fate.

"You know what? I want Bradley, as our newest member, to attach these chains"—Dirkson held up two chains—"to his brothers!" The people watching erupted into a joint laugh and cheer. Alistair shot a fearful glance at Davenport, who answered with an equally scared glance. Alistair craned his neck and watched as the crowds parted and Bradley slowly made his way up to Dirkson. Bradley took a deep breath and took the chains.

"Yes, sir." Bradley nodded and turned toward Alistair. Alistair felt his heart beat faster than he thought humanly possible and looked up pleadingly at Bradley, but he knew there was nothing Bradley could do. He had to follow Dirkson's orders, or he'd surely be shot. Alistair knew it wasn't fair to plead for his life, as it was useless. Alistair wanted Bradley to survive, and his survival rested firmly in his ability to follow orders. Should his cover be blown, it would kill them all in a single swift blow.

"I'm so sorry, Ally," Bradley whispered as he attached the long chain wound to the stake to the back of Alistair's handcuffs. He slowly turned and walked over to Davenport. Bradley's legs seemed weak, unable to carry himself plus the guilt of chaining up his brothers. Alistair felt sheer pain for his brother.

Alistair could barely hear Bradley whisper sorry to Davenport.

CHAPTER 17

The fleeting light gave way to an eerie darkness, and the sun crumpled to form the dust that danced within the moon's glow. The absence of light sent a chill through the air. Alistair hated the darkness. He was cold, tired, angry, scared, and dejected. He had tried for hours in a fruitless attempt to free himself from the chain, but the only thing he accomplished was draining his energy. At least the firing from the castle had ceased, leaving them in silence.

"How could he do this to us?"

Alistair sighed. "Davy, we've been over this. He had no other choice."

"He could've sacrificed himself for us."

"And then how would we escape? This isn't Brad's fault, Davy. He did what he had to."

"No, you're right. This isn't Brad's fault. It's yours."

"Mine?" Alistair was taken aback by his brother's accusation, but he knew Davenport didn't mean it. Davenport was just angry, and when he cooled down, he'd realize this was no one's fault.

"You killed Marcus."

"Davy, they were going to kill us either way—"

"You're prolonging the process."

"Davy—"

"Who's going to save us now? Who? You cared more about Tobias than me, you saved Tobias's life, but you can't save mine?"

Alistair flinched backward, collapsing into the darkness's arms. He was offended to his core; Alistair cared more about Davenport than he did about himself. He had dedicated his life to protecting his brothers, even as adults. Alistair was too stunned to speak. He had risked his life for Davenport, and he'd take a bullet for him in a heartbeat. Alistair turned away from his brother and sighed. *I'm a great brother*, he told himself. But he didn't know if he really was. It was he who had led his platoon to fight numerous battles, battles that got Colburn killed and Bradley shot. He had ignored Bradley's deep fear of flying and forced him into a plane. *No, I had to. . . .*

The thunderous sounds of heavy machinery boomed through the fields, and Alistair was almost out of breath. He and his men had been running from the larger German force for what seemed like hours, and everyone was struggling with the weight of the guns, ammo, and backpacks. Alistair swallowed his fear, as he knew they couldn't run much farther with all this weight holding them down.

"Ditch the guns! Drop ammo!" Alistair barked. He flung his rifle off his shoulder and tossed the ammo from his back into the bushes. Everyone did the same, as they knew they were running for their life, and the lighter the load, the better.

"Let's go!" Alistair watched as all his men resumed running, and he waited until everyone had passed him to continue. Should the Germans catch them, Alistair wanted to be the first to go. After all, he had led his men into a near ambush, so he should be the first to suffer the consequences. "Go! Go! Go!" he shouted.

The Germans were now close enough that he could hear their voices, and he was terrified they'd be gunned down. Then he heard the sound of planes above. Looking up, he let a little bit of hope leak into his heart as he recognized the aircrafts—British Bristol F2s—

maybe twenty of them. Alistair looked around and realized there was more than enough field for the planes to land and pick up Alistair's mere thirteen men. He didn't have the full force of his platoon because this was a highly classified, small reconnaissance mission, yet the enemy had somehow known they were coming. Alistair grabbed a flare from his boot, a tactic his training officer had taught him, and fired it.

"Help!" Alistair shouted. The pilots must've spotted the flare, because they all turned and began to circle his position. Alistair held his breath as the pilots began to flash a message using Morse code. *How many?* They asked. Alistair reached for his flashlight and flashed back *thirteen.* Alistair saw the planes send messages in Morse code to each other, then thirteen of the twenty planes lined up and began to make a risky descent onto the flat field just in front of Alistair and his men. The remaining seven circled their position, presumably providing limited air support.

"What's happening, Ally?" Brad asked.

"Bristol Fighters are two-seaters, but a lot of the time it's only one pilot per plane because it's more effective. We're getting in, it's our only hope."

"No." Bradley's voice was firm and harsh. He stopped running and just glared at Alistair.

Alistair stopped running and put his hands on his brother's shoulders. "Would you rather die?"

"I'm not going in a plane."

"Ally! Brad! Come on, quickly!" Colburn shouted for his brothers. Men were already hopping in, and the planes were quickly taking back to the sky, bound for the nearest base.

"Brad, please, Brad."

"No!" Bradley's voice quivered.

"I know you survived a plane crash, Brad. But it's the plane or the Germans."

"Neither."

"Bradley Jameson! Get in a plane right now or you'll die."

Bradley shook his head no. Alistair needed to get his brother in a plane, but clearly he wouldn't get in on his own free will.

"Ally! Brad!" Colburn cried. Alistair knew there was no other way to get his brother into a plane than with physical force. Sighing, he turned away from Bradley before suddenly turning back and striking Bradley with his fist. Bradley stumbled and collapsed into Alistair's arms. Alistair grunted as he grabbed Bradley's arms and dragged him toward the planes.

"Colburn, help me!" Alistair cried. His brother came running and grabbed Bradley's legs. Finally, they reached the planes just as the Germans came into view. Alistair could hear the shells from gunfire land just shy of his position.

"Get in the plane, I'll load Brad in the one behind you."

"You sure?"

Alistair nodded, and Colburn hopped in and the plane sped away. Alistair dragged Bradley to the next nearest plane and lifted him up and into the seat. He strapped his brother in.

"Is he okay?"

"Yes, he'll be fine. He will be terrified when he wakes up." The pilot nodded, and Alistair rushed to the final plane.

"Nothing like the last second." The pilot chuckled as he sped up his plane and the pair took off into the sky just as the Germans' fire landed only inches short of them. Alistair let out a deep sigh of relief. He only hoped Bradley would forgive him.

"Thanks." Alistair was out of breath.

"No problem, sir." The pilot sounded remarkably jovial for such depressing times.

I'm sorry, Brad, I'm sorry.

"I'm sorry, Ally."

Alistair lifted his head, startled by Davenport's voice. "Huh?"

"I shouldn't have said that. You are a great brother, the best brother anyone could want."

"It's all right, Davy."

"No, no, it's not. This isn't your fault, and it's not fair for me to take my frustration out on you."

Alistair smiled. For someone with a temper, Davenport knew how to be remarkably mature too. It was something Alistair often forgot about Davenport, and he kicked himself for not remembering. Davenport was trying his hardest to leave his old self behind and let pre-war Davenport reign supreme. Alistair knew, however, that that Davenport was gone forever, and only certain aspects of that Davenport remained. The rest died with Colburn.

"It's remarkably calm, the darkness." Davenport broke through Alistair's thoughts.

Alistair looked around; indeed the darkness brought forth an unusual peace. Alistair couldn't see anything, and that was calming; he couldn't fear what he couldn't see. If there was no light, did he even exist? If he couldn't see the dangers, did that make them arbitrary? "I thought you were scared of the dark."

"I am, but not here, not aboveground. I'm surrounded by nothing; my soul can fly free and take with it the fright of the unseen."

"What happened in those tunnels, Davy?" The silence that followed was somehow piercingly loud.

"Carnage," Davenport finally said. "Blood. Death. Fights. Explosions. Collapses."

Alistair sighed. Davenport never went into much depth about what had happened underground, but Alistair knew Davenport would have to tell someone before it killed him. Although, it may not get the chance to kill him.

"This could be worse, right?"

"I suppose. Ally, is there anything you regret?"

"Regret? Davy, we're not dying."

"Not yet."

Alistair paused and thought long and hard. There were many things he could regret, but he had learned to let go of those because they were only weighing him down, and he couldn't deal with them. There was one time though, one instance, where he could never forgive himself.

Alistair flung himself onto the ground.

"Get down!" he ordered. He was a young and inexperienced lieutenant, and this was only his second command.

"Sir, all due respect, but I don't think we should get down. I think we should keep moving, get as far away from the Germans as possible."

"Father Romano, when you hold a gun, you can make decisions. I'm the one in charge, not you."

"I'm aware, but—"

"But nothing. I've given my orders."

"Yes, sir." Alistair could hear the Father sigh and reluctantly hold his tongue. Bullets whizzed overhead, but it didn't sound as though the Germans were advancing. All of his men looked around, terrified. Then suddenly, the firing stopped, and all was quiet. Alistair slowly rose to his knees, confused by the sudden stop. Then he heard a German shout, *"Feuer!"* Alistair's heart froze and his fear spiked. Germans popped up from behind the bushes all around them and began to fire. Alistair could hear his men cry out as they were shot.

"Run to the north!" All his men, or those who were able, jumped up and sprinted dead ahead, firing as they did to clear the area, even though there were no Germans. Alistair's lungs burned; this was his first experience running for his life. After sprinting for what seemed like years, he slowed down and looked around. What he saw broke his heart: Of the fifty men he brought with him, he saw only eleven. The Germans had claimed thirty-nine of his comrades. He cursed in raw frustration.

"Let's keep moving. Is everyone okay?" The men with him nodded. Only a few had minor gunshot wounds, and the rest were shell-shocked, Alistair included. His breathing was fast and shallow, and he tried to calm himself for the sake of his men. He put his hands on his chest and took a few deep breaths until he could think clearly. He should've listened to Father Romano. If Alistair had chosen to run, no one would've been killed. Those thirty-nine lives were his fault, and he regretted it deeply.

"Father, I'm sorry. I should've listened to you."

"We all make mistakes, sir."

Alistair shook his head. His mistake cost him thirty-nine lives. "Not of this magnitude."

"Yes, of this magnitude. I bet you'll never make a mistake like this again."

Alistair glared at Father Romano. "Excuse me?"

"I mean, sir, that this will be the only time the majority of your force doesn't come back."

"And your point?"

"My point is that this catastrophic mistake is your first and last. You're young; for the rest of your career, you'll only have success."

Alistair rolled his eyes and focused on the rest of the survivors. They all walked in a dejected silence, some weeping, others too stunned to say anything. Alistair knew these men would never forget the events of what just happened, nor would he. The guilt of the lost lives had already clenched its jaws around his fragile heart.

"Alistair?"

Alistair lifted his anguish-filled head and scanned for whomever called out his name.

"Alistair?" Alistair breathed deeply and looked around.

"What?"

"What do you regret?"

"I killed thirty-nine of my men. It was the most I've ever lost. I should've listened to Father Romano, but I thought I knew better and ignored his advice. As a result, only eleven of the original fifty men I led survived. I'll never forgive myself for that."

"I'm sorry, Ally. But you had no way of knowing that would happen."

Alistair sighed and lifted his eyes up to the sky in an effort to stop the tears from flowing. Nothing Davenport could say would make him feel better. He knew those lives were on him and him alone. "What do you regret, Davy?"

"I regret . . ." Davenport's voice quivered and weakened. "I regret diving only for Bradley. If I had thought of it, I could've knocked Bradley into Colburn and saved them both—"

Alistair cut him off. "No way, Davy. I saw the whole thing. If you tried that, you all could've been killed. At the very least, Colburn and you would've been killed."

Unlike Alistair, Davenport couldn't put his regret behind him. While Alistair would never forget, he wouldn't let their deaths ruin his present soul. Every morning before breakfast, Alistair would recite the names of the men who died that day, and that was his way of coping and moving forward. Davenport, however, still clung to Colburn's death. Although, losing a brother is more painful than losing a hundred men.

"I don't think so."

"I know so." Alistair fumbled in the darkness, his hands still cuffed behind his back, and inched his way over to Davenport. He lay his head next to his brother's.

"We're going to die, aren't we?"

"There's always hope."

"You know what Nietzsche said about hope?"

"No."

"'Hope, in reality, is the worst of all evils because it prolongs the torments of man.'"

"Perhaps, but what else do we have to hang on to? Once we accept defeat and our spirits die, the body soon follows suit."

"Maybe we should accept death."

"There's hope, Davy."

"Hope, in reality, is—"

"I don't care about what Nietzsche said. He and I are not the same. Was he ever chained up?"

"Not that I know of."

Alistair sighed. "We should try and get some sleep before the sun rises."

"What's the point?"

"We need the energy, Davy. This is a direct order: Sleep." Alistair and Davenport chuckled harmoniously.

"Fine. Goodnight, Ally."

"Goodnight."

"Old soldiers never die."

"Old soldiers never die." Alistair closed his eyes and welcomed the drowsiness. He needed sleep, and he desperately wanted to dream. He wanted an escape from the real world, because even though he was preaching optimism to Davenport, he was, in reality, not optimistic. He didn't see a single outcome in which they survived. Alistair knew they had two more days and two nights left to live, but he wasn't ready to die. Maybe Nietzsche was right—hope is evil. Alistair felt himself slipping away into an exhausted sleep, yet with each ticking second, he came closer and closer to his own death.

CHAPTER 18

Alistair heard men off in the distance. He wasn't optimistic that his comrades would find them. He turned to see if Davenport had heard it, too, and his heart dropped. His brother wasn't there. Abruptly sitting upright, he saw Davenport's handcuffs on the ground. Alistair got up and scanned the horizon for his brother, but Davenport was nowhere to be found. Frightened and alone, Alistair felt his world spinning. He was overwhelmed and desperate, but worst of all, he had no clue where his youngest brother was. He bent down and pulled with all his might at the chain attached to his handcuff. He struggled and pulled, yet it wouldn't budge. Then finally, he heard the unmistakable sound of chain giving way and snapping. Alistair flew backwards and landed on his back with an ominously quiet thud. Slowly picking himself up, he noticed someone standing off in the horizon. He got up and waved his hands frantically. He opened his mouth to shout, but no sound came out. Frightened, Alistair took a deep breath and looked around again. The landscape felt different; it felt grizzly and ghostly. A thick fog began to roll in, followed by a chilling mist. Alistair shivered and fell to his knees in defeat. He was physically free, but he wasn't free from misery. Davenport was gone, and someone stood off in the horizon just watching him suffer. Was it one of the Snappy Kings? Alistair was confused, and his chest began to seize and he started coughing uncontrollably. Again and again he tried to call out to the man on the horizon, but again he couldn't say anything. He stumbled forward and collapsed onto his hands and knees and began a desperate crawl to the silent man. His fingers dug hard into the unforgiving soil as he pulled himself along with all his strength. He coughed and wheezed unrelentlessly; every breath felt like his last. Sweat pooled on his forehead and dripped onto his tired hands, stained with the despair of the overturned soil. He tried again and again to cry for help, but he couldn't make a sound. Suddenly, the fog lifted, and the sudden burst of light forced Alistair to look down. The silhouette of bloody uniform boots came into view, and Alistair slowly let his eyes trace the legs to the torso of the man. He had five visible bullet wounds, and when the man breathed deeply, Alistair looked up at his face. Alistair's chest tightened, and his brain refused to make his heart beat. He couldn't believe his eyes. He violently swung his head right and left, trying to shake the image, but when he stopped and jerked his head back up, the man he saw was the same.

"Colburn?" Alistair choked. There was no way that the man in front of him was his dead brother, it couldn't be.

"Alistair," Colburn responded in a ghastly voice. It rang off the eternal nothingness of despair and echoed deep into Alistair's soul.

"There's no way," Alistair cried. "There's no way." Alistair couldn't help himself. He dropped his head, and heavy tears flowed like mud out of his exhausted eyes. "Where's Davy?" Alistair climbed to his feet and rose, scanning the horizon for his youngest brother.

"I'm here, Ally. Focus on me."

Alistair shot his head back at Colburn. "How?"

"Don't question it."

"How, Colburn? I watched you, I saw you get shot, and I saw you collapse!"

Colburn just shrugged.

"No, no. I buried you, I spoke at your funeral. Old soldiers never die!"

"Never die is right."

"Colburn! What's happening?" Alistair took a step toward the ghostly figure of Colburn, yet he couldn't feel the warmth of life. "No, no, no! Colburn!" Alistair exploded into a crying fit. "You died!"

"If there's a will, there's a way." Colburn stood, perfectly still, never moving.

Alistair couldn't keep himself calm. He shook with the weight of a thousand men's woes, barely able to support himself. His head spun and his vision blurred. Then in an instant, Colburn was gone.

"Colburn!" Alistair shouted and whirled around in a desperate search for his brother.

"Alistair!"

Alistair turned and turned, but he couldn't find him.

"Colburn! Colburn!" Alistair shouted so loud, the back of his throat burned.

"Alistair!"

Alistair's panic peaked as he realized his brother's voice was full of terror.

"Alistair!"

Alistair fell to the dirt, overwhelmed, and fainted.

"Alistair!"

Alistair gasped and shot up like a rocket. Sweat dripped from his head and traced the ring of the handcuffs. He breathed quickly in and out of his mouth, trying to calm himself.

"Alistair?"

Alistair turned his head and was relieved to see Davenport sitting next to him, looking concerned.

"What's wrong?"

Alistair didn't know if he should tell Davenport, as Davenport had nightmares about Colburn's death regularly and Alistair didn't want to trigger them. "Nothing, Davy. Go back to sleep."

"Not until you tell me. You were screaming, Alistair. I think I'm deaf now."

"Bad dream."

"About?"

"Colburn," Alistair said after a while. "He was alive."

To Alistair's surprise, Davenport let out one long sigh.

"Davy, I'm sorry." Alistair was still worried he had upset his brother.

"No, no, it's not that. It's just that we're going to die and I'm going to spend my last days in a puddle of misery. I thought I'd be able to be a father. Can you imagine? A little me running around." Davenport woefully chuckled. "But now, no."

"I know what you mean." Alistair looked deeply upon the sun beginning to rise. "My poor Esme." With the rising sun came a little warmth, but nothing made Alistair feel warm. He was freezing and in pain, both physically and mentally.

"Was it incredible?"

"Was what incredible?"

"Esme's birth. I heard it really changes a man."

Alistair smiled with the warming memories of his daughter.

"Honey!" Alistair stopped Atlas and looked around. He thought he had heard his wife calling, but he wasn't sure. He leaned forward and stroked Atlas's long mane and powerful neck.

"Honey!" Alistair jerked his hand back to his side and turned Atlas around. This time he was certain he was hearing his wife calling.

"Pearl?" Alistair called as he galloped Atlas back to their home. He didn't have far to go, and he reached the barn quickly. To his shock, Pearl stood in the barn, doubled over and breathing heavily. "Pearl!" Alistair brought his horse to a stop and hopped off.

"Alistair," she huffed, reaching out for him, "something's wrong."

Panic spread through Alistair's heart as he rushed to his wife's side. "What's wrong?"

"The baby," she wheezed. "The baby is coming."

"Now?" Alistair was overwhelmed. "But you're three weeks early!"

"The baby is coming *now!*"

Alistair took three deep breaths, trying to calm himself. Pearl, on the other hand, began to get even more anxious. She grabbed at her back and took quick rapid breaths.

"Sit."

"On the ground?"

"I'll grab the birthing chair from the house." Letting go of her arm, he sprinted out of the barn and toward the house. He thrust open the door and dashed right to the kitchen, when he heard the sound of a motor outside roaring closer and closer. Jumping to the kitchen window and looking out, he spotted Bradley and Loretta.

"Bradley!" Alistair opened the window and waved his hands. Bradley, startled by the desperation in Alistair's voice, jumped out of the car and drew his gun. Alistair pushed away from the kitchen and burst out the front door, chair in hand.

"Put your gun away, Bradley."

Loretta calmly stepped out of the car and put her hand on her husband's shoulder. He shrugged her off.

"What's wrong, Ally?"

"Pearl—" Alistair struggled to get a word out. "She's–"

Loretta looked around Alistair and pointed to the barn. "Oh my god, she's gone into labor!"

Alistair nodded, and Loretta grabbed the chair from his hands and flew to the barn.

"Is she really?" Bradley holstered his gun, astonished.

Alistair nodded aggressively and grabbed his brother's arm as the two hurried back to the barn.

"You ready for this, brother?"

Alistair shot his head up at Bradley, both excited and extremely nervous. "Yes and no."

"Alistair! Get in here!"

Alistair and Bradley picked up the pace. Alistair blew past his concerned horse and rushed to his wife, who was gripping the chair she sat on so tightly her knuckles were white.

"For goodness' sake, don't just stand there," Loretta demanded. "Bradley Jameson, go get water!" Bradley nodded and rushed off.

"Thanks, Loretta," Alistair said.

"I'm not done yet. Come here and hold your wife's hand."

Alistair nodded and jumped next to his wife. "Loretta, do we need a doctor?"

Loretta shook her head. "Not enough time, Alistair."

"Not enough time?" Pearl shot her head up and grimaced. She wailed and fell back into the birthing chair.

Alistair's heart broke because he knew there was nothing he could do to dull the pain she was in.

"No, the baby is coming now."

"Loretta, we need a doctor."

"No we don't, Alistair. I'm a nurse, I know how to deliver a baby."

"When was the last time you delivered someone's baby?" Alistair locked eyes with Loretta.

She flared her nostrils, clearly offended by Alistair's comments. "While you men were off shooting people, someone had to step up and replace the doctors, Alistair. I delivered many babies. So unless you think you can do this yourself, sit there and comfort your wife!"

Alistair shook his head and bit his tongue. He realized Loretta was right, he had no idea what to do.

"Bradley! Give me the water right now." Bradley came jogging into the barn, careful not to spill a single drop of water. Loretta dabbed the end of her sleeve in the water and gently stroked Pearl's forehead.

"Let me." Alistair grabbed the water and dunked his sleeve and placed his wrist on his wife's head. She was sweating profusely, and Alistair worried that she would overheat. His heart was flooded with so much excitement, but his wife's cries of pain spooked him.

"How much longer?" Pearl gasped.

"Not much," Loretta replied calmly, "Keep pushing, Pearl!"

With his other hand, Alistair grabbed his wife's hand and instantly grimaced. She squeezed so hard, Alistair wondered if she broke one of his bones, but he didn't care. The pain he was feeling only made his concern for Pearl increase tenfold. He wanted to take away her pain, but this was something only she could do, and he felt a sense of pride that she was willing to go through all this for both herself and Alistair. Then Pearl began to breathe quicker, and she aggressively clenched her jaw, squeezing Alistair's hand even harder.

"You're so strong, Pearl." Alistair continued to stroke his wife's head with his wet sleeve, hoping it would cool her down. Pearl continued to cry out for several minutes while Alistair held her hand, and finally, he heard the joyous cries of his baby. Alistair dropped his wife's hand and rose from his knees slowly, in a trance-like state, hypnotized by his baby's first breaths of life. Bradley rushed behind Alistair and grabbed a clean cloth hanging on the side of a stable and gave it to Loretta. She swaddled the baby and looked up at Pearl and Alistair, smiling.

"It's a girl."

"A girl?" Alistair gasped. He felt lighter than he ever had. He floated next to Loretta's side and looked, for the first time, at his daughter.

"My sweet girl." Alistair had never felt such joy before as his precious daughter stared back at him. He didn't even bother to try and stop the tears from coming; they flowed freely, dragging out the sorrow within his soul and filling it with the purest form of joy known to man. He looked up at Bradley and jumped. "This is my daughter, look at her!"

Loretta leaned forward and gently placed the baby in the arms of her mother. The sight of his beautiful wife and pure daughter made Alistair glow.

"She's perfect." Pearl rocked the baby in her arms and looked up at Alistair, tears in her eyes too. Alistair went to his wife and placed his hand behind her head.

"She's more than perfect. She's our daughter."

Pearl looked from her new baby to Alistair and smiled. "Esme. I think Esme suits her."

Alistair laughed and nodded his head, too happy to even say a word.

Pearl laughed and stroked Alistair's cheek. "Oh, Alistair, you're crying more than me."

Alistair only glowed more. He leaned forward and kissed Pearl's forehead. "This is the best day of my life. Thank you, Pearl, and my sweet, sweet Esme." He reached his hand out and very gently rubbed his daughter's head. He had never been happier in his life.

"It was the best day of my life." Alistair glowed.

"You're crying, Ally."

Alistair reached up and felt the tears that flowed. Even just thinking about that day made him cry tears of joy. Esme brought only joy—natural, raw joy untouched and unstained by humanity. Somehow, her human soul encapsulated the best qualities of nature.

"I know." Alistair nodded his head and let the tears come. They weren't heavy or harsh, but rather light and airy. He wasn't ashamed to cry for his daughter like he was to cry over miseries.

"I really wanted to be a father, Ally. I was going to raise them like how our parents raised us—on horseback. My trusty Rouge would help teach my child to ride just like he had done for me."

"That's how I'm raising Esme." Alistair chuckled. "She loves to ride Daffodil, her little palomino Dartmoor pony."

"Ally, can I ask you something?"

"Sure."

"How do you know you're doing a good job as a parent?"

Alistair hesitated; the question caught him off guard. He didn't know for sure if he was doing a good job as a father, but he had to believe he was.

"Honestly, I don't know. But Esme is the brightest thing in my life, so as long as I'm keeping her shining, I know I'm doing something right." Alistair looked at his dejected brother. "Don't worry, Davy. One day you'll meet your child, I promise."

"I can't leave Cordelia to raise our child alone."

Alistair felt a pang in his heart and looked down to keep sadness from flowing into his eyes.

"Oh, I'm so sorry, Ally. I wasn't thinking."

Alistair shook his head and looked up. He was determined to keep the sadness out and Esme's joy in. "It's okay, Davy."

"No, Ally. I know how her death affected you. You didn't talk to anybody for weeks. Brad and I looked after Esme, but you never left your room."

"Not my best moment." Alistair remembered how the sadness made even common, everyday tasks difficult. Alistair solemnly chuckled.

"Not at all. Ally, what made you finally come out of your room? Brad and I tried nearly everything, but nothing we did worked."

"I heard Esme crying one night. I know you and Brad tried to calm her down, but little three-year-old Esme wasn't listening to you guys. I heard her cry out, '*I want my daddy and my mommy!*' and my heart shattered in two. I realized how selfish I was being, and I didn't hesitate. Her mother was gone and she needed her father, not her uncles."

"Oh, I remember that. Your hair was disheveled, your eyes swollen, and you didn't even have a shirt on. You looked like someone who had been lost in the desert for weeks," Davenport teased.

"Oh, come on." Alistair laughed. "I couldn't have looked that bad."

"Yes, yes, you could've."

Alistair looked at his brother and smiled. He almost forgot about their dire situation. He really came to appreciate Davenport in this moment: Here was his youngest, most fragile brother stepping up in a time of need.

"What?" Davenport noticed Alistair staring at him.

"I'm proud of you, Davy."

"Thanks." Davenport looked down, embarrassed. "Ally, I just want you to know that you've been an amazing brother."

"Davy—" Alistair was cut off by a sudden sharp pain in his wrist. He grimaced and looked down. The handcuffs trapping his wrists were beginning to tear into his flesh and cut off his circulation.

"What's wrong?"

"The cuffs are starting to get uncomfortable."

"I know, I know."

The silence that ensued was also uncomfortable. But there wasn't much left to say. Alistair knew he and Davenport were going to die; it was only a matter of time. The sunrise was beautiful, a complete contrast to the darkness surrounding Alistair and Davenport. He wasn't ready to die, he knew Davenport wasn't ready to die, and he knew Bradley wasn't ready to be the sole Jameson brother standing. There was so much at stake and so little hope. Alistair sighed and let himself collapse onto his side.

As the glistening sun rose, his dismal soul sank.

CHAPTER 19

Alistair could scarcely remember the events of yesterday. With no food or water and the threat of death looming, Alistair's mind was playing tricks on him. Now it was his last day alive. He was determined to make the best of the situation, even though he knew that would prove challenging. Indeed, there was no reason to smile, no reason to be happy, and no reason to be optimistic.

"Davy?" Alistair whispered and gently nudged his brother awake.

"What?"

"We're going to die today."

"Thanks for reminding me," Davenport responded dryly.

"Davy?"

"Hmm?"

"What was your happiest moment?"

Davenport angrily chuckled. "Are you being serious?"

"Yeah." Alistair looked his brother dead in the eye. He wanted Davenport to die remembering the best moments in his life. Poor Davenport dwelled in the darkness, and Alistair just wanted to remind Davenport of life with joy.

Davenport sighed, clearly exhausted.

"Come on, Davy."

"Riding Rouge after the war."

"He's a great horse."

"Yeah." The awkward silence soon crept back. Alistair was so scared to die, he didn't know what to say. During the war, Alistair grew closer to Bradley and, up until his death, Colburn. Alistair knew, however, Davenport was different; Davenport was a tunneler. Alistair turned and studied his brother carefully. Davenport stared off into the horizon, mindlessly focusing on the unimportant landscape.

"Davy—" Alistair cleared his throat. "You've got to let them out."

"Let who out?" Davenport remained looking blankly ahead.

"The memories."

Alistair saw a shift in Davenport's posture. He sat up straighter, clenching his jaw and rapidly moving his eyes up and down to force both the tears and the memories back. Alistair felt horrible because there was nothing he could do. He couldn't physically reach out and stroke his brother's back, and he couldn't help Davenport mentally as he didn't know the memories. Finally, Davenport shattered the thin silence.

"It killed me, Ally. I died under the battlefield years ago." Davenport began to sob.

"Shhh, it's okay, Davy."

"I remember the dirt suffocating my lungs, yet I'd dig. I dug with a shovel in my right hand and a knife in my left hand. Every so often, I'd stop and listen for the Germans. I'll never forget the first time I dug into a German tunnel. All I saw was blood, and all I heard were shouts. Blood over my hands, some of it my own, some of it the Germans'. It was awful, Ally, awful." Davenport tried to grab his neck, but the handcuffs prevented that. "I had my neck slit once. Have you ever been that close to death? My neck was slit, and I should've died. But guess who saved me? Roger Francois. He stuck his fingers deep into the cut to squeeze the blood vessel while simultaneously stabbing the German tunneler. I never thought someone could save a life and end one at the same time, but Roger did just that." Davenport paused and began wailing. Alistair's heart shattered. Clearly there was more Davenport was hiding, but he was happy that Davenport had finally started to open up.

"I've dealt with the constant stress, but then I had to deal with the stress of killing Colburn—"

"Davenport! You didn't kill Colburn. Did you fire the machine guns? Did you hide the explosives underneath our trench? No, no you didn't. I don't think anyone else would've been able to save one, Davy. You saved Bradley, and I doubt I could've saved one."

"Maybe."

"No, not maybe. Father Romano says even he wouldn't have had the foresight to bravely dash out of the trench and tackle Bradley."

"Father Romano is a hero."

"Perhaps, Davy, but so are you."

Davenport turned his head to the sky. After a while, he broke the silence. "I wonder how Tobias is doing. I didn't know how much he meant to you."

"He saved my life." Alistair didn't add that he saved Colburn's too.

"What's it like to be shot? I want to know before I feel it."

"You've been shot before."

"No, only grazed. I've never had a bullet lodged in my flesh before."

Alistair stopped to think about being shot. The worst instance was when he was shot at point-blank range. He still sometimes had pain as a result of that bullet wound.

"It's too calm, Alistair, too calm." Father Romano was standing watch with Alistair. Alistair had tried to convince Father Romano to go to sleep with the other men, but he refused.

"I know, I feel like something is wrong." Alistair turned to look at his platoon. All his men were asleep on the bare ground. They were tired from working their way back to England's trenches after their top-secret mission that resulted in Bradley shooting down German aircraft.

"Maybe we're just being paranoid."

"Do you really believe that, Father?"

Father Romano sighed. "No, sir."

"That's what I thought."

"Alistair, can I ask you something?"

"Sure." Alistair turned to look at Father Romano, slightly concerned.

"Why am I part of your platoon?"

"What do you mean?"

"I've been deployed with over ten different platoons within a matter of months, yet when you replaced Colonel Mack in this platoon, you didn't transfer me."

"You're vital, Father. Not all wars are fought with guns, and you keep me and my men sane. Without you, morale would be low, more men would be dead, and I would've requested a transfer only days in." Alistair put his hand on the Father's shoulder. "We need you." The Father smiled and looked down.

Suddenly, the night sprung awake on the heels of a gunshot. Alistair cried and collapsed to the ground; he'd been shot. He could smell the smoke from the gun, and he knew he'd been hit from point blank range. Everyone else woke up and jumped to their feet, guns drawn, and rushed toward Alistair, who rolled around in a pool of sheer agony and blood. With each breath, the pain increased, sending sharp waves cascading down his spine and into his lungs. His wound burned, and his blood felt hot. He yelped with every second that ticked, and he could feel his consciousness begin to waver.

"Ally!" Bradley shouted and flew to the wounded Alistair.

Alistair gasped for air. His chest squeezed and he felt fear, fear that he would die and leave his brothers alone. Alistair knew he couldn't die.

"Only one shot?" Bradley shouted.

"Yes!" Father Romano screamed, panicked.

Alistair's mind started racing as he realized someone wanted him and only him dead; one shot meant a sniper. Alistair tensed his body, and the pain rapidly increased tenfold. He gasped and cried simultaneously before he finally gave up and slipped out of consciousness.

"Ally?"

Alistair rapidly blinked to bring himself back to the present. "Painful. Being shot is painful." He drew a deep, long breath as he felt the pain of his bullet wound.

"Can you elaborate?"

"It burns, Davy, it burns like hell. Every breath you take feels like it could be your last, although you're no stranger to that"—Davenport chuckled—"and your vision blurs."

"I don't want to be shot, Ally."

"I know."

"It's funny. I could always boast about fighting the entirety of a war and only being nicked by a bullet, barely even a gunshot wound."

"Bet you never thought this is how you'd finally be taken down."

"No." Davenport slowly shook his head. "But at least I'm not alone."

Alistair lifted his head and solemnly smiled at his brother. He was happy he wasn't alone; maybe if he was, he would've already found a way to end his life before the enemy took it.

"I'm surprised we haven't frozen to death."

"Or died of dehydration."

"Yeah." Alistair looked toward the sky, grateful for the light rain the previous night. "When do you think Dirkson and company are going to come and shoot us?"

"No idea."

Almost as if on cue, Alistair heard the shuffling of boots coming toward them. The eerie sounds reminded him of the war—the boots, the laughs, the guns.

"Shhh, listen," the general said.

Alistair stopped dead in his tracks, turning to look at General Davidson. Fear wound its way around his spine, forcing tension through the heart of his nerves. He looked around slowly, not daring to even take another breath. The general grabbed his binoculars and scanned the horizon, pausing to study every tree. What the general saw, Alistair didn't know, but he could hear something coming. "What's that?"

"Shhh." Colburn shushed him.

"Boots." Bradley shuddered.

"Germans?" Alistair asked.

"No clue," Bradley answered.

"Silence." The general's stern voice brought forth a rapid quiet. Alistair swiveled his head around, but he couldn't see a thing. Yes, he heard the sound of men marching and laughing, but he couldn't see them, especially ducked beneath the top of a trench. "Alistair, come here."

Alistair jumped at the sound of his name. Surprised, he cautiously rose and made his way over to the general. "Sir?"

"Take these," General Davidson said and handed his binoculars to Alistair. "What do you see?"

Alistair hesitantly grabbed the binoculars and looked around. He couldn't see anything. "Nothing, sir."

"Exactly. Now look at the German trench."

Alistair turned his head and peered into the German trench opposite his position. He made eye contact with a German soldier who, just like Alistair, was looking around. "A German, sir. He's looking right at me."

"Exactly."

"Sir?"

The general sighed. "If the Germans are looking around, too, then it means those boots can't be German."

"Then what are they?"

The voices were getting closer and closer. The general grabbed his pistol and cocked it. Then, he lowered his gun.

Puzzled, Alistair looked around.

"They're Russian."

"Russian? What are they doing here?"

"No idea."

Suddenly, the sound of gunfire crackled across the otherwise somewhat calm scene. Alistair dove to the ground, placing his hands over his head. The general rolled his eyes and grabbed Alistair by the back. "Get up."

Alistair lifted his face away from the dirt and looked around. He hadn't heard a second gunshot.

"Get up, soldier."

Embarrassed that he dove to the ground after only a single gunshot, Alistair rolled over onto his side.

"Get up!" Alistair's mind jumped to the present again. His wrist felt oddly light for the first time in three days. He looked down and saw that the handcuffs that once trapped his wrists were off.

"Get up!"

Alistair shook his head, startled, and jumped to his feet.

"Took you long enough, Alistair. I could've just shot you now."

Frightened, he registered the three men, perhaps three barbarians, that surrounded him. "Dirkson," Alistair grumbled.

"Get a move on, Alistair." Dirkson shoved Alistair forward, and he weakly took three steps to get in line with Davenport, who was being forced forward by Cromwell. Alistair turned to look at his brother and noticed Davenport was silently crying. Alistair understood; he didn't want to die.

"To your knees!" Cromwell barked.

Alistair collapsed to his knees and watched as Davenport did the same. There was no point in fighting.

"Hands on your heads!" Eastaughffe ordered.

Alistair breathed deeply as he slowly and shakily raised his hands. He stared at the grass and heard someone maniacally waltz in front of him.

"Look at me."

Alistair raised his head and saw Dirkson standing tall in front of him and Davenport, who was also kneeling with his hands on his head. "Well, this has been exciting. Alistair, I've enjoyed fighting you. Life is more fun with a challenge. Unfortunately, all good things must come to an end, and this is yours. Davenport, it's been nice knowing you. Your end has come too." Dirkson signaled with his hand, and Alistair heard Cromwell and Eastaughffe cock their guns behind them. Dirkson smirked. "Any last words?"

Alistair looked at his brother and nodded. Davenport cleared his throat and strongly declared his last words.

"Old soldiers never die." Davenport's strength poured out and painted his final four words. Alistair tearfully met his brother's gaze. Davenport woefully nodded, and Alistair managed a smile plagued with the despair of death.

"Old soldiers never die." Alistair looked at his brother one last time and lowered his head, closing his eyes. He could feel Colburn's presence waiting to greet him.

"Very well. Cromwell, Eastaughffe, on my call."

Alistair breathed deeply as he tried to reconcile his death.

"Three . . ."

Alistair heard Davenport sigh. Neither brother was ready to die, especially not like this.

". . . two . . ."

Alistair tried his best to connect with his emotions, tried to pull the joy from the depths of his soul.

". . . one . . ."

This was it. Alistair knew he'd die in the next second. His mind began to play the drama of his life, and Alistair realized how long of a life he'd lived. Physically, his life had been short, but mentally, it was long. The war had drained him and added years to his life, and Alistair looked forward to finally being free from the strain of those added years. In the nanoseconds he had left to live, he finally accepted his fate and relaxed his tense muscles.

". . . fire."

Bam. Bam.

The rest was silence.

CHAPTER 20

All was white, all was calm. For the first time, Alistair felt no guilt, no fear, and no shame. There was an unnatural amount of peace, and he had no clue whether he was in the natural or human realm; all he knew was that he felt light. Instead of flooding him with memories of the war, his brain flashed him images of young Colburn running around, riding horses, and giddily playing the piano. Alistair smiled; he had forgotten Colburn loved to play the piano. He remembered standing in the doorway of the music room, watching his younger brother play the piano with such grace and such elegance that Alistair slid to his knees. The notes grabbed him and swept him through the gentle harmony, letting Alistair feel calm. Alistair wished he had more time with Colburn, more time to listen to Colburn's piano, and more time to laugh with all his brothers. Alistair grinned at the thought of seeing Colburn again, yet he frowned at the thought of leaving Bradley behind. He also frowned at the thought of leaving his precious daughter an orphan. Esme was the unfortunate victim of his poor actions, or lack thereof. But he need not dwell on the darkness, because he was surrounded by light. The dark drenched his soul in a taxing, heavy misery, but the light showered his soul in a relieving lightness and peace, peace that Alistair had longed to feel again. The war robbed him of that ability, yet now he could breathe. The mental fatigue that encased his soul was broken and for the first time he felt free. Alistair felt like he was flying, and certainly he was weightless. And then it all came crashing down.

"Alistair!"

Alistair's eyes flung open, and the light fled instantly. In came the darkness of reality. Alistair had never been so overjoyed to see the dark.

"Alistair!"

Alistair cleared his throat and looked up. Dirkson stood in front of him, hands in the air, glaring dead into the soul of someone behind Alistair.

"Alistair!"

Alistair shot his head to his left. There was Davenport, resting on his knees, trying to catch his breath. Shocked, Alistair slowly rose to his feet and turned around. The sight he saw caused his jaw to drop. There, lying in front of his feet, lay Oliver Eastaughffe. His gun rested in his hand, which was closed and limp. His head lay on its side and it donned an entry and exit point of a single, sharp bullet. Oliver Eastaughffe was dead. Turning, he saw the same sight behind Davenport: Frederick Cromwell was dead, sprawled out on the ground in a pool of his own blood. Alistair could still smell the gunpowder, and he looked up to locate the source. There, standing with a gun aimed right at Alcott Dirkson's head, stood Alistair and Davenport's savior. A smile, a genuine smile, spread across Alistair's face. He took three big steps toward his savior and paused, whispering Davenport's name. Davenport lifted his head and turned around. The second Davenport saw the two dead, he jumped to his feet and rushed to Alistair's side.

"Thank you, thank you." Davenport choked on his words. "I'll be able to meet my child."

"Did you really think I'd let my two brothers die?" Bradley laughed. Alistair felt his heart melt; Bradley had saved them.

"Brad, Brad . . ." Alistair couldn't even think of what to say. "Thank you, my fearless brother, thank you, thank you." Alistair's eyes teared up, but he quickly swept the tears away, as there was still some unfinished business to attend to. Alistair nodded and Davenport rushed into the arms of their savior, while Alistair grabbed the gun and turned back to Dirkson.

"Well, Mr. Dirkson, looks like you're all alone." Dirkson grumbled but said nothing. Alistair chuckled, a deep, powerful, guttural snicker. He had the power now; he had Dirkson begging for his life.

"This seems unfortunate, doesn't it? Tell me, what's stopping me from shooting you, hmm? Because I could kill you right now."

"Now, Mr. Jameson, let's not be animals. You don't need to kill me."

"That's right, Dirkson. We've won, so what better time to set the terms than right now?"

"Mr. Dirkson," Bradley stepped forward, "did you really think I'd ever betray my brothers? How gullible are you?"

"You were branded." Dirkson spat.

"Yes, yes that's true, but it's just a scar, a constant reminder of our victory and your defeat."

"You . . . You almost killed my brother. You almost killed me!" Davenport snarled and lunged toward Alistair, trying to grab the gun from his hand. Bradley stepped forward, restraining him from getting any closer to the gun. They didn't want to kill Dirkson; they wanted him alive so he could always remember his defeat.

Dirkson grinned. "You're still so immature and impulsive, Davenport. Can't you just grow up?"

Alistair breathed deeply in through his nose and out through his mouth, calming himself down. "Let's go, Davy, Brad. He's not going to challenge us again." Alistair glared deep into Dirkson's soul. "He's leaving town, didn't you know? He can go clean up his mess first, though. But us, tonight we celebrate like kings! Tonight we go home to our families and to our horses. Go, go Mr. Dirkson, get out of here." Alistair flicked the gun and Dirkson scowled before trotting off. Smiling wide, he grabbed his brothers close. They had done it, they had won; Conwy was all theirs. Alistair swung his arms over Davenport's and Bradley's shoulders, and the three brothers triumphantly began their march back to Conwy. Suddenly, Alistair stopped and turned around.

"Oh, Mr. Dirkson!" Alistair let go of his brothers and took a few steps closer to Dirkson, who stopped and reluctantly turned to face Alistair. Alistair turned his head and signaled for Dirkson to rest his gaze upon a log. "That fallen tree was once a sight to behold. It used to stand tall and proud, yet it came crashing down to earth. Ironic, isn't it?"

"What's ironic, Mr. Jameson?"

"Oh, how the mighty fall."

ABOUT THE AUTHOR

Grace Godfrey was born in Rhode Island in 2005 and at age three moved to the North Shore of Boston, where she has lived ever since. Two years ago, at age sixteen, she began writing her novel, *The Mighty Fall*, in her dorm room between classes and homework, and she just kept on writing. Godfrey is currently completing her junior year of high school at Fusion Academy, where her favorite class is history. In her free time, she loves going on walks with her puppy, Hamlet, and watching the Boston Bruins. This is her first book.

www.ingramcontent.com/pod-product-compliance
Lightning Source LLC
LaVergne TN
LVHW101320110826
845152LV00014B/156/J
* 9 7 8 1 9 5 1 5 6 8 3 5 1 *